How to Take the
Ex Out of
Ex-boyfriend

How to Take the Ex Out of Ex-boyfriend

Janette Rallison

G. P. Putnam's Sons

G. P. PUTNAM'S SONS
A division of Penguin Young Readers Group.
Published by The Penguin Group.
Penguin Group (USA) Inc., 375 Hudson Street, New York, NY 10014, U.S.A.
Penguin Group (Canada), 90 Eglinton Avenue East, Suite 700, Toronto,
Ontario, Canada M4P 2Y3 (a division of Pearson Penguin Canada Inc.).
Penguin Books Ltd, 80 Strand, London WC2R 0RL, England.
Penguin Ireland, 25 St. Stephen's Green, Dublin 2, Ireland (a division of Penguin Books Ltd.).
Penguin Group (Australia), 250 Camberwell Road, Camberwell,
Victoria 3124, Australia (a division of Pearson Australia Group Pty Ltd).
Penguin Books India Pvt Ltd, 11 Community Centre, Panchsheel Park,
New Delhi—110 017, India.
Penguin Group (NZ), Cnr Airborne and Rosedale Roads, Albany,
Auckland 1310, New Zealand (a division of Pearson New Zealand Ltd).
Penguin Books (South Africa) (Pty) Ltd, 24 Sturdee Avenue, Rosebank,
Johannesburg 2196, South Africa.
Penguin Books Ltd, Registered Offices: 80 Strand, London WC2R 0RL, England.

Published simultaneously in Canada. Printed in the United States of America.
Design by Katrina Damkoehler. Text set in Stone Serif.

Library of Congress Cataloging-in-Publication Data
Rallison, Janette, 1966–
How to take the ex out of ex-boyfriend / Janette Rallison.   p. cm.
Summary: Giovanna rashly breaks up with her boyfriend Jesse when he refuses to
help her twin brother with his campaign for Student Council president, but fixing
her mistake may be more difficult for her than she realizes.
[1. Dating (Social customs)—Fiction. 2. Elections—Fiction. 3. Popularity—Fiction.
4. High schools—Fiction. 5. Twins—Fiction. 6. Brothers and sisters—Fiction.
7. Stepmothers—Fiction. 8. Schools—Fiction.] I. Title.
PZ7.R13455How 2007   [Fic]—dc22   2006026543

ISBN 978-0-399-24617-3
1 3 5 7 9 10 8 6 4 2
First Impression

*To James and Faith—my wonderful twins—
and also to my other magnificent children,
Arianna, Luke, and Asenath.*

*To the real Dante and Giovanna Petrizzo,
you all have such cool names.*

*To my ever-patient and thorough editor, Tim.
Okay, so while I was working on your revision comments I
compared you to the Greek Furies and told several people you
were possessed by evil demons. I still followed most of your
suggestions. You're great. Thanks for making the book better.*

Special thanks to Brandon Hart, Brian Lamb, and Angela Morales
from the Austin, Texas, police youth service department for guiding me through the
intricate legal world of frog theft.

Thanks to all my writing friends who read and critiqued parts
of the story. You guys are not only talented but helpful.

Lastly, thanks to Asenath's friend Westin, who came over
on short notice so I could drag him around in a cowboy hat to pose
as Jesse. Keep the hat handy, Westin, it works for you.

Chapter
1

I bet you Cinderella didn't get along with Prince Charming's friends. Oh sure, the knights and barons probably put up with her on account that she was pretty and had such dainty feet and all, but you know every duchess and countess in the kingdom hated her guts. That's how women are when someone encroaches on their turf.

And that's why all the girls at Jesse's birthday party ignored me. While he mingled with the guests to make sure everyone had enough food, I sat next to a group of cheerleaders who talked around me like I was a piece of furniture.

I don't know why I expected any different. They'd acted this way since I started dating Jesse two months ago, giving me subtle and not so subtle messages that just because I was going out with a guy from the popular clique didn't mean I fit in with them.

It wouldn't have been so bad if I'd been sitting with Dante, and then I'd at least be able to talk with him, but he stood across the room, his black leather jacket barely visible in the crowd of letterman jackets. He and a bunch of guys from the basketball team were no doubt talking sports, and other male languages I didn't understand. Besides, I ought to be able to make it through a party without depending on my twin brother as a conversational crutch.

Next to me on the couch, Bridget and Stacey—the current reigning rodeo princess and her peroxide blond sidekick—discussed their prom dresses. They hadn't said a word to me all night except for when I sat down and Stacey said, "Oh, hi, Giovanna." She said my name like it had about seven syllables. No matter how many times I've told her it's pronounced "Geo-vonna," she always finds a way to butcher it. If I correct her, she laughs and says, "Sorry, I don't speak Italian."

Yeah, neither do I, but somehow I manage to pronounce my name without making it sound like it rhymes with "banana." I won't even mention how people say my last name, Petrizzo, except to point out it has stumped many a substitute teacher during roll call.

Dante says I should take advantage of my Italian heritage and pretend to be a non-English speaking immigrant whenever we have a sub, but that's just Dante. He's never taken school seriously.

Bridget took a sip of her drink and leaned toward Stacey. "I brought home this gorgeous blue silk dress with a sequin bodice. It totally matched the color of my eyes, but my mom freaked out because it was so low cut. She insisted on taking it back and going with me to pick out another one. I chose the most expensive one in the store to make her mad."

Stacey let out a sigh. "I wish I'd thought of that. I had to beg my mom before she let me spend over three hundred. And I still haven't found a pair of shoes."

I shrugged. "I haven't even looked at prom dresses yet."

Bridget's gaze turned to me for the first time. Her eyebrow lifted. "Why not? Hasn't Jesse asked you?" She gave me a self-satisfied smile. "Maybe he's going to ask someone else then."

I gripped the drink in my hand harder than I needed to. "I'm sure he just hasn't gotten around to it."

Bridget let off a giggle as she rolled her eyes. "You don't need to be so touchy. I was just kidding."

Stacey fingered the straw in her glass. "Of course he'll ask you—that is, unless he finds something better along the side of the road." And then they both laughed, so if I got mad they could claim they were just joking around again.

You see, Jesse and I did sort of meet by the side of the road. Oh, I'd known who he was. It's hard to overlook tall, gorgeous guys, but I'd never talked to him. Bickham High isn't a big school, but it's well divided. Jesse is captain of the basketball team, and thus firmly part of the in crowd.

I might have never spoken to him if Dante's motorcycle hadn't broken down. Dante had just bought the bike a few weeks before, a secondhand Yamaha that probably should have been compacted into paperweights instead of sold. Dante thought he could fix it up, and assured me the engine would not explode on our rides to or from school. And it didn't. It wheezed to a stop one afternoon after school, fifty feet outside of the Bickham High parking lot.

He tinkered with his bike—tinkered in this case meaning smacked things while swearing—and I stood around watching people's facial expressions as they drove by.

The popular kids got a real kick out of seeing us stranded on the side of the road. A few of them honked in passing. Then Jesse pulled up to us and stopped. Jesse rides a motorcycle too, although his is a new, sporty-looking one, unlike Dante's, which may have been fished out of a lake at some point. Between the two of them, Jesse and Dante got the bike working again, and have been friends ever since.

This, by the way, is the only benefit I've so far seen to having a twin brother. They bring home hot friends to work on their bikes in your garage.

"Where is Jesse?" Bridget asked, craning her neck to look around the room. "He certainly hasn't spent much time with you tonight. Guys can be so bad that way. You know, paying attention to other girls when you're not around."

Whatever. I smiled even though I wanted to throw my drink at Bridget. "Maybe I should go find him."

I got up without saying another word to either of them and walked into the kitchen. It was empty. Which was probably a good thing, because if Jesse had been there, I would have unloaded on him about how his friends were all jerks. And I told myself from the very beginning I wasn't going to do that. I wouldn't make him choose sides.

Instead, I picked up some chips and chomped a few angrily while I tried to convince myself, again, that Stacey, Bridget, and the rest of the popularity brigade just needed more time to get used to me. Eventually they'd accept me, if not for my sake, then for Jesse's.

I also tried to convince myself that his friends weren't completely evil. Jesse liked them, so they must have some redeeming qualities.

Then again, they never openly snubbed me when Jesse was around—maybe he just didn't realize that Stacey and Bridget couldn't assemble a redeeming quality between the two of them.

While I dumped more potato chips onto a plate, Dante

strolled into the kitchen. "Hey Giovanna, when do you want to leave?"

"I can't leave Jesse's party. I'm his girlfriend."

"Then you'll have to find another ride home, because I'm going."

I held one hand out to him, pleading. "Don't leave me here by myself. Jesse is your friend too."

"Which is why I showed up. I came. I ate. I'm leaving. If you hang too long with this crowd, you can actually feel your brain cells dying off."

"Well, at least people are talking to you."

Dante grabbed a handful of M&Ms and tossed a couple into his mouth. "Oh sure, and I can never hear enough stories about Wilson's last skiing trip to Vail, or how difficult it is to be in the student council."

For a moment I worried on Jesse's behalf. "You didn't insult Wilson, did you?"

"Insult him? I couldn't even get a word in edgewise. Every time he shut his mouth long enough, some girl or another jumped in to ask him a stupid question that made him start talking again." Dante tossed another M&M into his mouth. "Why do girls like listening to that crap, anyway?"

Because Wilson is six foot three inches of good looks with shoulders like a linebacker, which I'm sure come in handy when he plays football as—let me think—a line-backer.

But Wilson isn't simply another jock. The boy gets straight A's. I know because he's in some of my honors classes. And did I mention his father, Wilson Montgomery Senior, is the mayor?

I'm not sure how much mayors make a year, but if it isn't a whole lot, then someone should audit the town's books, because Wilson drives a BMW to school.

So why do girls hang on Wilson's every word? I believe the scientific explanation would involve a discussion on hormones, chiseled jawlines, and an analysis of the typical teenage girl brain.

"I don't know," I told Dante.

Jesse walked into the kitchen. "There you are, Gi. I've been looking all over for you."

Dante grabbed some more M&Ms and headed to the door. "Hey Jesse, great party. Thanks for inviting me, but right now I've got to . . ." Dante waved his hand in an upward spiral. "You know, do some stuff . . . so see you on Monday."

"Thanks for coming," Jesse said, but he didn't take his eyes off of me.

Jesse is exactly what I pictured cowboys would look like when I moved to Texas three years ago. Mussed brown hair, broad shoulders, and biceps that could be used to wrestle steers to the ground. Plus he wears cowboy boots half the time. Seriously. He has a casual and a formal pair. He also has aqua blue eyes, which are capable of stopping time when he looks at you.

The clock paused for several minutes while he walked toward me, smiling. "Are you having fun?"

"Yeah."

"Then how come you're hiding out in the kitchen?"

For a moment I considered telling him about my conversation with Stacey and Bridget, but even as the thought ran through my mind, I dismissed it. I wouldn't criticize his friends at his birthday party. "No reason. I'm just going through the chips to see if I can find one that looks like Jay Leno."

Jesse stood close to me. "I know why you're really in here, and I'm sorry."

"Are you?" Had he heard what Bridget and Stacey had said to me? I brightened up at the thought. I mean, that would make things so much easier if he saw for himself what they were like.

Jesse took the plate from my hands, laid it on the kitchen counter, and took my hands in his. "Sorry I've ignored you. I've been so busy running around trying to make everyone feel welcome I've barely talked to you, but I'll make it up to you."

"Really?"

"Yep, I promise not to have another birthday party for an entire year."

I squeezed his hand. "It's sweet how you sacrifice for me."

He pulled me toward him, then bent down to kiss me. I held my breath, waiting to melt like I did whenever we were close, but just then a couple of Jesse's basketball buddies walked into the kitchen.

One of them cleared his throat in an exaggerated manner, and the other said, "It looks like Jesse's birthday wish already came true."

I pulled away from Jesse and laughed in what I hoped was a casual and perhaps slightly sophisticated manner, but I felt myself blushing bright red.

Jesse grinned. "Don't mind us. We're on our way out." Then he pulled me out the kitchen door and back into his family room. We plopped down on the love seat, and I noticed Dante hadn't left after all, but stood a few feet away talking to Wilson, Bridget, Stacey, and Wilson's best friend, Luke Talbot.

"Everyone thinks student council is just about planning dances," Wilson said, "but it's more than that. People don't see all the work that goes into it, or the decisions we have to make."

Dante let out a grunt. I could tell from his posture

he was in one of his the-popular-kids-are-idiots moods. "When was the last time student council decided anything important?"

Wilson took a sip of Coke. "Today. Our budget was lower than expected, so we had to cut some things in order to have funds for next year's homecoming float. It wasn't easy. I hate to break it to everyone, but instead of serving soda at prom, you all get punch." He laughed as he looked over the group. "Probably the watered-down kind."

"Yeah, that's important stuff." Dante snapped his fingers as though remembering. "Whatever happened to the memorial the student council was doing for Norman Pike?"

"That was one of the areas we cut."

"You cut the memorial for Norman?"

Wilson took another sip of his drink and shrugged. "I told you it wasn't easy."

Norman had been killed in a car accident last month. I hadn't known him that well, but Dante and he had done a social studies project together sophomore year.

Dante's eyes took on a stubborn glint as he looked at Wilson. "Homecoming float? You want to spend money for a trailer that someone shoves pieces of crepe paper onto, but not for a memorial for one of the students?"

Bridget, who is also in the student council, shook her head at Dante like he just didn't get it. "We sent a plant to his funeral. It's not like we did nothing."

"Oh. A plant. Well, it's nice to know that if I die to-night, the students of Bickham High will comfort my family with a fern."

Jesse forced a laugh and called over to them, "Hey Dante, if you die, I'll personally see to it that Giovanna's comforted with more than a fern."

"Right," I added. "Plus I'll also get to keep all of your stuff." I expected Dante to throw some comment back at me. Or to laugh—something that would break the tension. But he didn't. He stared at Wilson.

"So does our class get to vote on the theme for the float?"

Which was when I knew Dante wasn't going to let go of the whole memorial thing. I mean, he couldn't possibly care about the float. Dante only goes to the occasional football game, and then spends most of his time making fun of the cheerleaders. His only comment on the float our class did this year was, "Hey, let's drop this baby in a river and see if it really floats."

Wilson smiled, but it didn't look like he meant it. "The class always votes on two or three possibilities."

"Great. I make a motion that the theme of our next homecoming float is 'Our student council was too cheap to do a memorial for Norman Pike, so we're dedicating this float to him.'" Then Dante looked at me. "Giovanna, do you second that?"

As he said this, everyone in the room looked over at me. I could feel the heaviness of their gazes on me and automatically shrank further into the couch. It was just like Dante to drag me into his fight with Wilson, but I couldn't leave my brother standing there without any support. I sent him a stiff smile. "Sure. I second the motion."

Bridget rolled her eyes. "It's too bad, then, that neither of you is on student council, and this isn't a meeting." She gave a tinkling little laugh and shrugged her shoulders. "It's not that I don't agree with you that every dead guy needs his own float, but we've already chosen the school theme. It's 'Bickham Tigers rule.' And we have three choices for our class float. The first is 'We've got a tiger in our tank.' The second is 'Cats always land on their feet'—you know, like we'll have one of our football players standing on a bunch of players from the other team, and . . ." She shut her eyes. "Oh, I can't remember the third one."

Wilson took another sip of his drink. "It's 'Has the cat got your tongue?' "

Bridget nodded. "Right. We thought we could have a tiger pouncing on a player from the other team and ripping his face off."

Luke laughed like this was somehow funny. "So there will be a dead guy on the float after all. You can call him Norman and dedicate the float in his memory."

I turned to Jesse to see his reaction to this. He groaned and shook his head, but I didn't know if it was because Luke was an insensitive dolt, or whether he just didn't like the float idea.

Dante smiled at Luke stiffly, then turned his attention back to Wilson. "The floats won't be built until next fall. Why is this year's student council already making the decisions?"

"We like to be prepared. It makes it easier to get everything ready."

Dante raised an eyebrow. "Doesn't next year's student body president get a say on what the theme is?"

Stacey, Bridget, Luke, and Wilson all glanced at each other and smirked. Wilson said, "Oh, definitely."

Which made Stacey and Bridget giggle.

Jesse called over to Dante, "Elections are in three weeks, and as far as anybody knows, Wilson is the only one running."

Bridget nudged Wilson with her elbow as though it were an inside joke. "It wouldn't matter if anyone else ran. Wilson would beat them."

"Which is why no one else is running," Stacey said. "Ain't no two ways about it." And then the four of them smirked again.

Dante smiled. "I'm running."

Bridget laughed, shaking her head, but Wilson's eyes narrowed. He stared at Dante, unspeaking.

Dante took his keys from his jacket pocket and strode to the door. "See you at the polls," he said, and then left.

As soon as the door clicked shut, all eyes turned to Wilson. He shrugged and smiled, evaporating the tension that filled the room. "Looks like I might have competition after all." Wilson raised his glass as though offering a toast to Jesse's guests. "And may the best Texan win."

A rumble of laughter rolled around the room, and Wilson's gaze followed it, silently accepting their support. Then his eyes stopped on Jesse. Something flickered in his expression. Perhaps worry. Perhaps a challenge.

The next moment, he turned back to Luke, talking and laughing so casually that I wondered if I'd imagined the look he'd sent Jesse.

Jesse stayed with me for most of the rest of the party, but we didn't talk about the election again until everyone left. Then while he put on his jacket so he could take me home, I looked out the window and thought about my brother. "You don't think Dante will really run for school president, do you?"

Jesse zipped up his jacket. "I doubt it. Most likely he was blowing off steam on account of the memorial for Norman."

Maybe, or maybe Dante just wanted to pick a fight with

Wilson. Over the years we'd lived in Bickham, Wilson had said some things about Dante, specifically that he looked like he shopped at only the best yard sales. And Dante had said some things back to Wilson, most of which were unrepeatable in polite company. So maybe Dante just wanted to fight.

"He might be upset about the memorial," I said, "but I don't know. It's not like he and Norman were close friends."

Jesse took my hand, and we walked toward his garage. "Remember how, not too long before he died, Norman tried to convince Dante to join the math team?"

I grunted, and Jesse held up a hand to stop my protest.

"I know—Dante's favorite thing to do in calculus class is to pretend like he's sleeping, but Norman told him he was smart enough to help out the math team. You don't forget that kind of thing."

We walked into the garage, and Jesse hit the button on the wall to open the door. It gave a protesting grind as it lifted to let the night air in.

I crawled onto the back of Jesse's bike and snapped on my helmet. "So is Wilson mad at Dante for saying he'd run?"

"Nah, and all that stuff Wilson said at the party about crushing Dante like a brittle walnut was just guy talk."

"What? Did he really say that?"

Jesse laughed and sat down in front of me. "It will all blow over by tomorrow. By Monday neither one of them will even remember that Dante said he'd run."

I held on tightly to Jesse's waist and hoped so.

Chapter

2

Twins are supposed to have a psychic connection. You know, feel each other's pain, recognize what the other is thinking, wake up in the middle of the night with premonitions if one is stuck down a well or something. Let me say right off this has never happened between Dante and me. When we were younger, I hoped it would. Occasionally I would try to use ESP to get him to share his dessert with me.

Maybe it's because Dante and I aren't identical twins. But it's more likely because Dante isn't trying hard enough.

This is what Dante's probable reaction would be if ever awakened in the middle of the night by a premonition:

Mystic Inner Voice: Dante, wake up, Giovanna needs you.

Dante (*grumbling*): What? (*He rolls over and tries to get*

back to dreaming about motorcycle engines or whatever it is
that occupies the empty spaces in his brain.)

Mystic Inner Voice: Get out of bed. Your sister is in trouble.

Dante: Yeah, she's always in trouble. Don't wake me up again unless you've got interesting news.

Mystic Inner Voice (*fading*): She needs your help . . .

Dante (*pulling the covers over his head*): It's probably some girl-trouble stuff, and I refuse to talk about clothes, guys, or anything that's found in the feminine hygiene aisle. Let Gabby deal with it.

Gabby is our stepmother, but she's so annoying I'm sure her inner voice has stopped speaking to her. Besides, if I were stuck down a well, Gabby would probably make me clean it before she pulled me to safety.

The only one in the family who would worry enough about me to get up in the middle of the night to check on me is the cat. Which might be the reason he occasionally jumps onto my bed and steps on my face. He's making sure I'm still breathing.

Anyway, Dante and I aren't psychic-bond close, but we're still there for each other. So when Dante brought up the election over breakfast the next morning, I very lovingly said, "Are you crazy?"

He sat back in his chair, leaving his bagel untouched. "You don't think I could win?"

"I don't know why you'd want to. Since when do you care what goes on in student council?"

Dante leaned forward again. "It's time we stopped letting Wilson and the rest of those . . . Aztecs run the school."

Aztecs is code for another A word which we are not allowed to say in the house because Skipper, our five-year-old half sister, repeats everything we say. And yes, her name really is Skipper, like the Barbie doll and that fat guy on *Gilligan's Island*. I have no idea what Gabby was thinking of when she gave her daughter this name, and I just count my blessings Gabby didn't marry my dad until long after I came along. Otherwise I'd be walking around saddled with a name like Gidget or Buffy.

Anyway, Skipper sat at the kitchen table beside us, humming and shoveling Cheerios into her mouth.

With a glance in Skipper's direction, I said, "Yeah, but even if Wilson and the other Aztecs didn't win the election, they'd still run the school."

Dante ripped off a piece of his bagel and tossed it in his mouth. "Maybe not. A lot of people at school are tired of all Wilson and his friends' . . ." His gaze slid over to Skipper. "Shellac. The students are ready for a change."

Well, I was certainly tired of the shellac thrown in my direction, but I hadn't noticed that my opinion had a lot of company. I took a couple of bites of cereal, feeling the intensity of Dante's stare on me the entire time.

"You know you'd like to see Wilson and his pals eat some humble pie," he told me. "So will you help me campaign?"

I shook my head. "Dante, don't do this. You'll just make everyone mad at you and me, and then you'll flake out halfway through the election and decide you don't want to run after all."

He sat up straighter in his chair. "When have I ever flaked out about anything?"

"You flaked out about tennis. Remember how you were all fired up about learning how to play, so Gabby enrolled us both in lessons?"

"Yeah."

"After two weeks you sneaked off with Lisa Jones during every lesson instead of playing. Meanwhile I got stuck playing Julie I'll-serve-it-down-your-throat Segner. I came home every afternoon covered in welts."

Dante grinned, and his voice took on a reminiscing tone. "I didn't flake out. The reason I wanted to take tennis lessons was so I could sneak off with Lisa."

I pointed my spoon at him. "How about swim team, then?"

"Cute lifeguards," he said.

"I got up every morning at six and swam laps in a cold pool so you could flirt with the lifeguards?"

Dante shrugged.

"So why are you running for president? Have you decided girls like politicians?"

He rolled his eyes at me. "I don't need to find ways to meet girls." True. Dante is six feet tall and has wavy brown hair and dark brooding eyes. Even some of the popular girls check him out when he walks by. Not that any of them would ever admit it. Jesse's friendship isn't enough to grant Dante full entrance into the world of the in crowd.

"You know why I want to run," he said. "Wilson is a jerk, and Norman needs a memorial. Simple as that. Are you going to help me, or will I have to explain to everyone why I don't have the support of my twin sister?"

I took a bite, glaring at Dante over my cereal bowl. "Sure, I'll help you. Even though it will make all of the popular kids hate me forever, and I know I'll regret it before the election is over, I'll help you."

He smiled at me. "Great. I'm going to ask Jesse to be my campaign manager today. If you see him before I do, hint that you'll only keep dating him if he agrees, okay?"

"Oh, see—I regret it already."

Dante held up a hand and laughed at me. "All right, I'm just kidding, you can date whoever you want."

I looked at Dante, pleading. "Don't drag Jesse into this. You know he's one of Wilson's friends."

"Yeah, but everybody at school likes Jesse. He's not

stuck-up like the rest of the popularity posse. If he's on my side, I can win this thing."

Dante was right. If Jesse helped him, he might have a shot. I still didn't like the idea, but I knew I'd have to try and persuade Jesse to help Dante. And I already had a date set up with him. We were meeting for lunch at Country Burger that day.

All that morning while I mopped floors and cleaned toilets, I worried about how to convince Jesse to be Dante's campaign manager.

I had a lot of time to worry about it, because on this Saturday morning, like most Saturdays for the last three months, I cleaned Bickham's Parks and Rec Center—chipping away at sixty hours of a community service sentence. It was a verdict Judge Rossmar had given me without really listening to my side of story.

You know that saying "Innocent until proven guilty"? Well, it turns out they don't need a lot of evidence to prove you guilty, especially if you do stupid things to incriminate yourself along the way.

But really, none of it was my fault.

Well, okay, maybe some of it was my fault.

The school counselor, who I am still required to check in with on a monthly basis, keeps telling me I need to take responsibility for my actions. She says a bunch of other stuff I mostly ignore because I'm not really a juvenile delinquent. I'm just a person with convictions. Unfortunately I'm now a person with convictions in both senses of the word.

See, last semester in biology class—for some reason I never fully understood—the teacher required us to dissect frogs. Mr. Clement told me it was so I could learn about internal organs. But here is my question: Don't we already know what frog organs look like? They dissected frogs last year, and the year before. Didn't someone already sketch out this vital information?

Mr. Clement refused to see the logic behind my argument. He also refused to see my point that I was absolutely certain I would never in my life need to know what a frog spleen looked like. Very few people do. He gave me an F for the unit and sent me to in-school detention for the period.

Normal parents would have called up the bio teacher and protested, or pled my case or something. After all, it was my father who gave Dante and me a tadpole habitat when we turned eight years old. So he at least should have understood that a girl who had pet frogs named Bert and Ernie was not about to slice one open.

But he had completely forgotten the No-you-can't-have-a-puppy-but-here's-a-tadpole-habitat pets. Instead he told me, "Start worrying about your grades and stop worrying that the world might have to do without one more frog." Gabby, of course, said more than that.

I listened to her go on for a week about how I'd never get into a good college because I'd skipped out on my biology dissection unit, and what was the big deal about dead frogs anyway? Dead frogs weren't scary. They didn't bite. Never once had there been a case of a dead frog who'd reached out his slimy little amphibious hand and grabbed a bio student by the throat.

The actual school detention wasn't that bad. I met many interesting people there, including a guy named Tim Murphy that I suspected to be an escaped convict who was just hiding out in high school to throw off the police. He showed me all of his body piercings, most of his tattoos, and sent me several notes suggesting we run off to Aruba together.

I declined on the Aruba thing, but when he offered to get back at Mr. Clements by breaking into the biology room and stealing the frog corpses, well, I laughed and told him it was a sweet gesture.

As it turns out, you shouldn't joke around with escaped convicts. The next day after school, a ziplock bag of dead frogs showed up in my locker.

My first reaction, of course, was to fling them on the

floor and scream. My second reaction was to find Tim, grab him by his eyebrow studs, and explain to him that, yes, women like to be surprised with flowers, but not dead frogs.

I didn't do either of these things, however, because I was too busy being grossed out to the point of nearly hyperventilating.

When I could finally breathe normally again, I decided the best thing to do with the frogs was to put them some-place where everyone could see the results of the senseless frog slaughter. The trophy case in the front lobby would work, and Dante could unlock it. I knew this because he and two of his friends broke into it once. They put one of Skipper's Barbie swimsuits on a little man that stood on one of the football trophies.

I would take the frogs home, write an unidentifiable essay on the value of life, then put them all in the trophy case the next day.

That was my plan, anyway.

When I got home, Gabby yelled at me half the eve-ning. It started out as a lecture on leaving my stuff in the living room, but quickly progressed into a treatise about how I didn't take my responsibilities seriously. From there she slid into the You've-ruined-your-chances-to-get-into-a-good-college-over-frogs routine.

So I slipped the ziplock bag into Gabby's briefcase. I

wasn't trying to be awful. I just wanted her to understand how sickening it feels to see dead animals that have been killed for no reason.

The next day Principal Nelson called me into the office as soon as I got to school. It turned out the frogs weren't the only thing stolen from the biology room. Nearly two thousand dollars' worth of computers and biology equipment was also missing.

With hands folded firmly on his desk, Principal Nelson stared at me. "Did you break into the biology room yesterday?"

"No," I said, but he must have seen the panic on my face. He leaned forward, his eyes narrowing in on mine.

"I'll ask you again, young lady, and I want you to think very hard about your answer. Did you break into the biology room?"

"No," I said.

He shook his head with disbelief. "Who else would have stolen dead frogs so that none of the students could complete the dissection assignment?"

"I don't know." Which wasn't entirely a lie since suddenly I wasn't sure it had been Tim. He wouldn't have put the frogs in my locker if he had also stolen computer equipment, would he? That would be like admitting he'd done it. No one would be that stupid.

Maybe it was someone who was trying to frame him. Or me.

I clutched my hands together in my lap. Thank heavens I hadn't put the frogs in the trophy case where they could dust the whole thing for fingerprints. The school had no evidence on me. All I had to do was sit still and keep professing my innocence.

The principal's secretary popped her head into the office. "Mrs. Petrizzo is here."

The next moment Gabby strode in, her heels clicking across the tile and the briefcase grasped in one hand.

"What are you doing here?" I choked out.

She shot the principal a sharp look, then sat stiffly in a chair. "That's what I'd like to know. I have a busy work schedule and don't have time to come to school every time there's a problem in biology."

The principal turned his stern gaze toward Gabby. He summarized the situation to her, then added, "We thought it best to involve a parent in this discussion. This isn't a prank. Stealing school property is a serious legal offense."

I didn't have time to answer, because Gabby jumped in. "You don't really believe Giovanna broke into the biology room and made off with a bunch of equipment? How would she have carried it home? Wouldn't someone have noticed a computer sticking out of her backpack as she walked out of school?" Somewhere from inside Gabby's briefcase, her cell phone rang.

"Don't get that," I said, but Gabby didn't even acknowledge I'd spoken.

"Besides," she said as she reached her hand in to her briefcase, "we couldn't even get Giovanna to touch a dead frog to save her GPA, so there's no way on earth she broke into the bio room and stole any—"

Gabby didn't finish her sentence.

Apparently in the jostle of coming to school, the ziplock bag had opened and spilled dead frogs inside her briefcase.

And okay, I'm sure it was a shock, but you'd think after all those Never-has-a-dead-frog-reached-out-his-slimy-little-amphibious-hand-and-grabbed-a-bio-student-by-the-throat speeches she gave me that she would be the last person to shriek uncontrollably and fling her briefcase so hard that several frog cadavers went flying into the air and onto the principal's desk.

Which they did.

So anyway, that's why I clean the bathrooms of the Parks and Rec building every Saturday morning.

It didn't matter that I finally told the principal everything I knew about the incident. Tim denied it, the missing equipment was never found, and when two people give the police different stories, they tend to believe the one who didn't accidentally chuck evidence onto the principal's desk during her interview.

To make a long and totally unfair story short, I was charged with possession of stolen property. Besides all of the community service I have to do, I'm on probation until I'm eighteen, and I had to pay a four hundred dollar fine.

Thank you very much, Tim.

You'd think that somewhere along the line, one of my fortune cookies would have warned me about all this. You know, given me a little slip of paper that said, "No good will come from convicts bearing gifts of dead frogs." But no. The fortune cookie industry has totally overlooked that message. Ditto for horoscopes.

I was so upset about the whole thing I didn't want to go back to school, not even after my school-imposed sentence of a month at an alternative learning center ended. But my dad kept telling me that if I didn't go back, people would think I was guilty. So I returned to school and a life that would never really be the same again.

Not many guys would ask out a girl who has henceforth been known at school as "The Frog Avenger," but Jesse did. He accepted my innocence casually, as though it didn't take any effort to believe in me. Which meant it would be that much harder for me to ask him to be Dante's campaign manager.

I'd never wanted to make him choose between his friends and me, and here I was about to do just that. And what if he didn't pick me?

Chapter 3

When I finished scrubbing out toilets, I pushed the cleaning cart back into the supply closet, and Earl checked off my work. Earl is the compulsively grouchy head janitor. Any other person would have shown a little cheer at the fact that I came in to do his job every Saturday, but no, he watches me like I might be secretly shoving rolls of toilet paper in my purse.

I drove to Country Burger, and Jesse and I ate lunch in a booth with the scenic view of the parking lot. Which is one more reason why it's nice to date a totally hot guy. Scenery becomes unimportant. We talked about school, friends, and that sort of thing. I didn't work my courage up to discuss the campaign until we were almost done with our meal. Finally I said, "Dante is serious about running for school president. He talked with me about it this morning."

Across the table from me, Jesse tilted his head in surprise. "Really?"

"Wilson has lots of friends, you know, people who'll help him with his campaign. Dante doesn't have as many—but you're his friend, aren't you?"

Jesse tapped his knife against his plate. He knew where I was going with this, and I could already see the hesitancy in his eyes. "Yes, I am, but I'm also Wilson's friend."

I leaned forward and tried to look beguiling. "Dante needs your help more, though, and you know he'd be the first one to help you if you ever needed anything. So will you help with his campaign?"

Jesse gazed back at me, his blue eyes softening. He didn't answer.

I reached out and put my hand over his. "Please?"

Jesse let out a sigh. "Dante put you up to this, didn't he? He knew I couldn't tell you no."

I smiled. "*No* is such an ugly word. You really shouldn't say it."

Jesse laughed, and intertwined his fingers with mine. "All right. I'll help Dante campaign. It will make things awkward between Wilson and me for a while, but sure, I'll help Dante."

With that one sentence, my hope surged. "Can you be Dante's campaign manager?"

All the laughter left Jesse's countenance. I could sense

him tense up. He took his hand away from me and ran it through his shaggy brown hair. "I don't want to make things that awkward. I'll help, I'll wear a button, whatever, but I can't be campaign manager."

"But Jesse—"

He didn't let me finish. "You should do it, Giovanna. You're his sister."

"He wants you."

Jesse shook his head again, this time with one of those knowing looks he gives me when he thinks I'm selling myself short. "You can do it. You can get out there and rustle up votes for him."

"Campaign managers should be movers and shakers. I don't really move or shake. And the whole frog thing—"

"Has blown over," he said. "No one cares about it anymore. It's not like people sit around and talk about you."

Which just goes to show you he hasn't been in the girls' locker room recently.

I tried one last time to make him understand. "Later today Dante is going to ask you to be his campaign manager."

Jesse shrugged. "I'll explain to him why I can't. I mean, I see Wilson all the time. He'll probably be at the library fund-raiser tonight." Jesse leaned forward again, his attention back on his food instead of me. "Don't forget, I'm picking you up at seven."

The fund-raiser would consist of mingling with a bunch

of old people, hearing a speech from the mayor about the importance of reading, and then some songs by Bickham High's choir. Jesse and I were only going because his mom was the choir director. She'd given him tickets and some not so subtle hints that he'd better come to support her.

I hadn't considered the fact that Wilson would be there too, but seeing as how his dad was giving a speech, it made sense.

Jesse's cell phone rang. He took it out of his jacket and looked at the caller ID. "Speak of the devil. Wilson is calling me now." But then he slipped the phone back into his pocket and went back to eating.

"You're not going to answer it?"

Jesse shook his head as he swallowed. "Not when I'm out on a date with you."

Which was such a sweet thing to say that I forgave him for refusing to be Dante's campaign manager.

"I'll call him later," he went on. "Wilson probably just wants to talk to me about tonight."

Maybe. But suddenly I was very glad Jesse had already agreed to help Dante before Wilson had a chance to speak to him.

When I got back home, I told Dante what Jesse had said about being his campaign manager. He grunted but said, "I'll talk to him about it."

An hour later Jesse called, and then Dante left with his motorcycle and a bunch of tools. He didn't return until I was cleaning up the dinner dishes. The dishes are always my job—Gabby's orders—even though Dante is perfectly capable of placing things in the dishwasher. My parents never make him do it because, "Dante does the yard work." I would point out that the lawn needs to be mowed once a week and we eat dinner every night, but to tell you the truth I don't mind that much. My strongest memories of my mother are seeing her in the kitchen, gliding between the cupboards, the stove, and the table.

She would talk to me while she cooked, her eyes on my face more than on the food in her hands. Even now, nine years after the cancer has taken her, I still feel closest to her in the kitchen.

While I rinsed plates off in the sink, Dante strode into the room smelling of motor oil. He grabbed the milk from the fridge and drank straight from the carton.

Skipper looked up from her place at the table, where she was currently exiled until she finished her meal. "You're 'posed to use a cup," she called to him.

"And you're supposed to eat all your food," he said back.

"How did things go with Jesse?" I asked.

Dante finished the last of the milk, crushed the carton, and threw it into the trash can. "Your boyfriend is an Aztec."

"He is not." I dropped silverware into the dishwasher with a noisy clang. "You can't blame him for being friends with Wilson."

"Yes I can. Wilson is a jerk, and Jesse is helping Wilson, not me."

Well, that was a bit of an overstatement, since Jesse had only turned down the position of campaign manager. I didn't have time to say this, however, since Dante went on. "You know what the most important thing to Wilson is? Wilson. He would steamroll over anyone to get what he wants—even Jesse. I just don't know why no one else sees that."

"Look, I can be your campaign manager." Even as I said these words, I couldn't believe they'd come out of my mouth. I didn't even want Dante to run for president, let alone want to be his campaign manager, but I didn't want Dante mad at Jesse either. "I can get my friends to help. Besides, you wouldn't want Jesse to be in charge of your posters anyway. I mean, we've both seen his handwriting, and half the time it could pass for hieroglyphics."

Dante leaned up against the counter and surveyed me silently for a moment. When he spoke, the anger had left his voice. "I don't want this whole thing to cause problems between Jesse and you. You don't have to get mad at him on my account."

I slid a couple of plates into the dishwasher. "Why would I get mad over this?"

"Because you're way too emotional, and you overreact about everything."

"No I don't."

"The last time you got mad, you put a bag full of stolen dead frogs in Gabby's briefcase."

I shrugged. "Only once."

Skipper turned away from her plate and toward us. "What did you put in Mommy's briefcase?"

"Nothing," I said. We've never told Skipper about the whole biology break-in incident. This is because Gabby doesn't think she's old enough to understand—which translates into We-must-hide-Giovanna's-bad-example-so-Skipper-doesn't-follow-her-criminal-ways. "Shouldn't you be off somewhere playing?" I asked.

"I'm 'posed to sit here until my dinner is gone." She rested her head in her hands and didn't lift her fork. Apparently she was waiting for Rumplestiltskin to come and do the job for her.

Dante walked to the table and picked up Skipper's plate. "You're done with dinner. Now go play."

"Dante—" I said.

"Oh, come on. She didn't eat it when it was warm. You think she's going to eat it now that it's congealing on the plate?"

Skipper looked at me hopefully. I took the plate from Dante's hand. "All right. Go play."

By the time I'd disposed of the casserole down the sink, both Skipper and Dante were gone. I decided to call Jesse and get more details of their meeting, but as I picked up the phone, Gabby walked in to survey my work.

"The sink needs to be wiped out, and don't forget to sweep."

"I won't."

"Where's Skipper?"

I glanced at the table. "Um. She left."

Gabby put one hand on the counter. Her long, red acrylic nails tapped out an accusing rhythm. "Did she finish all of her casserole?"

How is it that Dante always knows when to disappear, and why is it that whenever I break the rules, I always get caught? Any other night Gabby would have forgotten she sentenced Skipper to a permanent place at the table. But no, not tonight.

Now if I said *yes,* Gabby would probably go lean on Skipper until the kid squealed out the truth. If I said *no,* Gabby would yell at me for not making Skipper eat her casserole—which, I might point out, was this bean and rice dish with cooked tomatoes floating around that no kindergartner on the planet would willingly fork into her mouth.

"She was eating it," I said, "but when I cleared off the table, I accidentally bumped her plate and knocked it on the floor. She couldn't finish it after that, so I told her to go play."

Gabby drew in a quick breath as though stung. For a moment I thought she knew I'd lied and was about to yell at me. Which would be my luck. But instead she swore and rushed to the garbage can. "Did you break my plate? Don't you know how expensive those are?"

"It didn't break," I said.

She shoved the garbage can back in its spot underneath the kitchen sink and turned with her hands on her hips. "Well, next time be more careful."

Gabby then went on to tell me, but I will spare you the boring details, the entire history of her dish collection, which she bought in England and which she can't get replacements for unless she pays, like, twenty dollars a plate, and that's without the shipping.

After that she walked across the kitchen, looked under the table, and told me I hadn't cleaned up all the mess. "I can tell where the casserole landed, and there's still a spot on the tile. You can't just sweep over that. You have to get the mop and wipe it up all the way."

So yeah, this completely put thoughts of Jesse and the campaign out of my mind, because I was too busy wondering what sort of psychological disorder causes people to see messes that aren't there. I also wondered why in the world we ate off of her precious dishes if she was so worried about them, and then I wondered how much trouble I'd get in if I, say, slipped the next time I unloaded the dishwasher and dropped three or four of them. Really hard. Across the room. Exactly what would a person have to do to make that look convincingly accidental?

At seven o'clock Jesse came by to pick me up for our date. He'd changed his jeans and cowboy boots for Dockers and loafers, and it amazed me that he could look equally stunning in both. Perhaps it was the effect of his aqua blue eyes contrasting against his dark hair. His eyes always seemed deep and mysterious.

Jesse smiled as I opened the front door. His gaze flickered over me, then he nodded in approval. "Well, don't you look fine." He always said that no matter what I looked like, but I still loved hearing it. Maybe it was the Southern drawl. He could make anything sound sultry.

I hadn't done much with my hair. Just put two clips in the sides to make it look like I had tried to go a little formal. All my friends say they wish they had my wavy brown hair, but that's only because they don't have to tame it into hairstyles.

Since I wore a dress, we drove to the fund-raiser in Jesse's dad's truck instead of on his motorcycle. To tell you the truth, that was a relief.

Oh, it's not that I don't love smashing my hair into a helmet as much as the next girl, but I can't shake the feeling that motorcycle riding is only a little more safe than, say, swimming in shark-infested waters while wearing a Spam bikini. I mean, when you ride a motorcycle, you can actually see the street moving beneath your feet—and it's going by really fast. It sort of reminds you how painful it would be to crash into the road at high speeds, and how quickly it could happen, since you're riding on a vehicle without a floor.

I so prefer riding in things that have floors.

We pulled into the Bickham Marriott, hands down the nicest hotel in town, and went into the conference center ballroom.

A bunch of people who I didn't recognize, because they were all about twice my age, stood around talking and laughing. Well, actually, I recognized Jesse's mother in one corner, but Jesse didn't seem to have any desire to go over and talk with her, which was fine with me. Even though Jesse denies it, his mom doesn't like me. I can tell by the way she grits her teeth together when she smiles at me.

I think she expected Jesse to go out with some Southern belle with a soft drawl and Texas pedigree as long as his. Instead she got the school criminal. I mean, all of the teachers look at me differently now—like I might be tempted to break into their classrooms in search of more dead animals to confiscate—so I can't really blame her for being less than thrilled that I'm dating her son.

Jesse and I picked up some hors d'oeuvres, then walked around the room. A few miscellaneous teenagers milled about, probably brothers and sisters of the choir kids, but no one I knew well enough to go up and talk to. Then we saw Wilson and Bridget across the room.

Wilson held up a hand to wave us over, and Jesse took hold of my elbow and steered me in their direction.

Bridget smiled at Jesse as we walked up. "Well, don't you clean up real nice."

Bridget isn't officially going out with Wilson, so she can get away with flirting in front of him. They went out for a while last year but supposedly are just friends now. Jesse told me this was her choice, not his, but Wilson has dated enough other girls since then that he doesn't appear to be all that heartbroken over the matter.

Jesse smoothed out a wrinkle in his khaki pants. "Thanks, but my jeans are a lot more comfortable."

She let her gaze run over him. "I bet."

I stepped closer to Jesse and then took hold of his hand, just to remind her that he was my boyfriend.

Bridget's eyes flickered over to mine, and she gave me a hollow smile. "It's too bad Dante didn't come tonight. Maybe hearing the mayor speak could teach him something about politics. After all, he seemed so interested in the subject."

I knew she was trying to provoke a response from me, so I just shrugged. "He's busy with other things."

"Of course, Wilson can learn all he needs from his daddy. Campaigning runs in his family. Runs and wins." She laughed, her shoulders gently shaking up and down, which was a dangerous thing since she wore a strapless dress. Personally, I'd be afraid to wear something that looks like it would slide off if you simply twisted the wrong way, but she is obviously braver than I am.

Wilson said, "If there's one thing I've learned from my dad, it's that you need the right people out there pulling for you." He nodded toward Jesse and Bridget. "You, my friends, are the right people, and I thank you for it." Wilson's gaze passed over me momentarily, and then he turned to Bridget. "I almost forgot to tell you. Jesse agreed to be my campaign manager."

Chapter

4

I stared at Wilson. The words made no sense. I waited for him to say the rest of it—the part with the punch line that would let everyone know he was just joking. Because he couldn't be right. Jesse had already agreed to help Dante.

But as Wilson went on talking about the election, Jesse didn't contradict him. I looked at Jesse's face, expecting to see surprise or confusion—something that would signal that Wilson had made a mistake.

Jesse wouldn't look back at me.

And then I knew it was true. The pieces fell together in my mind. The call from Wilson, the fact that Dante had been mad at Jesse when he'd come home. He'd even said, "Jesse is helping Wilson, not me." But I hadn't understood. I hadn't realized Jesse had jumped candidates.

I suddenly felt cold. My lips involuntarily clamped

together like they'd been glued shut. Oh, I had a lot of things I wanted to say, but they seemed lodged in my throat. I couldn't say them with Wilson and Bridget standing inches away.

I clutched my glass and stared at the floor. How could Jesse do this to me after I'd asked him to campaign for Dante and he'd said he would?

Wilson finally turned to me. "So, Giovanna, are you going to help Jesse work on my campaign?"

I didn't say what I thought, which was, "Obviously your tie is too tight, because it has cut off circulation to your brain."

See, sometimes it's a good thing to keep your feelings bottled up inside you, no matter what the school counselor says. I forced a smile. "No, I'm Dante's campaign manager."

He raised an eyebrow. "So he's really running?"

"Yes. Why wouldn't he be?"

Wilson took a slow sip of his drink. "Well, it just seemed like one of those 'Big hat, no cattle' kinds of announcements."

"I guess you don't know Dante very well then."

Bridget's gaze skipped back and forth between Jesse and me. "A boyfriend and girlfriend working on opposite campaigns. That ought to make the elections more interesting this year." She giggled and nudged against Wilson. "You'd better watch out that your manager doesn't leak all your secrets to the enemy camp."

"We have secrets?" Jesse asked. "I must have missed that meeting."

"We have no secrets, only strategies," Wilson said. "And I'm sure none of them are worth stealing." Then he gave me a dazzling smile, which I had seen before but never directed at me. "I think right now our number one strategy should be to convince all the pretty girls at school to vote for me." He nodded in Jesse's direction. "I'll let you use your powers of persuasion on this one. I expect you to have her turned around by the end of the night."

I smiled back at Wilson and once again refrained from making comments about his tie or oxygen supply. Jesse put one hand on my back, but I still couldn't look at him.

Mrs. Shappel, who worked at the downtown library, walked over to the microphone and invited everyone to take a seat by the stage.

Wilson and Bridget headed in that direction. I didn't move. Jesse gave my elbow a gentle tug. "Let's go find a seat."

"I want to go home."

"We can't go home now. It would be rude. It would look like we just came for the food."

I still didn't move. My throat felt tight, and it hurt to

swallow. "How could you agree to work on Wilson's campaign?"

Jesse gave a sigh and dropped my elbow. "Didn't Dante tell you about this? I thought he was going to." Jesse's eyes grew soft, but I turned my head so I wouldn't have to look at him.

"I asked you this afternoon to work on Dante's campaign and you told me you would."

"Can we talk about this later?" Jesse looked over my shoulder at the stage. "We need to sit down. Wilson's daddy is about to speak."

Well, we couldn't offend Wilson's daddy. I followed Jesse to the seats. Most of them were taken. I saw a few empty chairs wedged here and there among the crowd but couldn't imagine crawling over everyone to get to them. After a moment's search, Jesse led me up front to two empty seats right beside the speakers.

I sat stiffly, staring up at Mayor Montgomery but thinking of Dante—which was hard to do since the mayor's voice boomed at me in this thunderous you're-sitting-too-close-to-the-speaker sort of way.

Jesse didn't try to talk to me again until the mayor sat down and the choir stood up. Then he leaned over and whispered in my ear. "Look, I'm sorry you're sore about this. I already explained it to Dante, and I thought he'd tell you. I owe Wilson a favor, and this is how I'm fixing to pay it." He reached over and squeezed my hand. "Trust me on this one, Gi. I have to campaign for Wilson, but it doesn't mean you and I will be fighting against each other. We'll keep our campaigning friendly; we'll use good sportsmanship. Everything will be fine."

"A favor? That's it? You owe Wilson a favor?"

"Right." He turned to the speaker again as though this closed the matter.

"You mean, like, maybe you borrowed Wilson's tools to work on your bike, or maybe he helped you put on your new handlebars or something like that?"

Jesse sighed and looked straight ahead.

I tried to ask more details, but the choir started up, and their singing muffled my words. Every time I spoke, Jesse asked, "What?" so I kept raising my voice. "Why do you owe Wilson a favor?"

"I can't tell you."

"Why not?"

"I don't want to talk about it."

Okay, so now he was keeping secrets from me. Great. The choir finished their song. We all clapped, and they started up the next song. Jesse sat up straighter and away from me, so it was harder for me to talk to him. I imagine he thought that would end the conversation, but I leaned over toward him. "You shouldn't pay back a favor if it means stabbing Dante in the back while you do it. I mean, is he your friend or just someone you hang out with until one of your popular friends comes along?"

Jesse's tone sharpened. "That's not fair. He's my friend, but he's got no chance of winning. And he's only running because Wilson said something that set him off. Besides, everyone still sees him as a newcomer."

A woman who sat in the next row gave us a stern look and mouthed the word, "Hush." I noticed a couple of other people scowling in our direction.

I lowered my voice. "Dante has lived in Bickham for three years."

"Exactly," Jesse said. "Wilson's family has been here for generations."

I could have pointed out that my dad's mom, Grandma Petrizzo, has lived in Bickham for the past twenty years, but I really didn't see why that should matter. Instead I whispered, "What exactly does the student body president do that requires generations worth of knowledge?"

"Look, I didn't say I agreed with it. It's just the way it is."

"All the more reason for you to help Dante instead of turning your back on him."

Jesse looked firmly at the choir onstage. "It's only a student election, all right?"

My stomach twisted. He cared more about upsetting Wilson than he cared about Dante—or me. I felt tears pressing at the back of my eyes but refused to let them form. Instead I folded my arms and let out a slow breath. "By the way, Jesse, your friends are jerks."

His head tilted in surprise. "What?"

"I didn't tell you before because I didn't want to make you take sides. But you did anyway. You chose them."

Disbelief flashed across his expression. He leaned closer to me and lowered his voice. "I'm not choosing between you and—" He let out a frustrated breath. "What do you mean my friends are jerks?"

I answered him in quick staccato rhythm. "If Bridget and Stacey were any faker they could pass for mannequins. Luke has the sensitivity of a bucket of rocks, and Wilson is so arrogant he not only thinks he'll win the presidency, he expects to be anointed king."

Jesse folded his arms. "You don't know the first thing about Wilson."

"He has next year's student council agenda planned before the elections have even happened."

The lady in the next row sent more shushing in our direction. Jesse leaned closer to me and mouthed, "You don't know Wilson."

"Well, one of us doesn't," I hissed back.

The muscles tensed in his jaw. "You're overreacting about this."

"I'm not overreacting."

"And you're being a tad too loud."

"Fine. I won't talk to you. Ever again."

His eyes narrowed. "What?"

I wasn't sure whether he couldn't hear me because the choir had crescendoed into a really resounding part of the song, or whether he was so cocky he couldn't believe that I would ever dump him. You know, me—the outsider, breaking up with multigenerational him. I raised my voice to make it clear for him. "Jesse, we are over!"

Unfortunately, as soon as I'd said the word "Jesse," the choir stopped singing. Without the speakers blaring, my words filled the room. Half the audience turned around to see why I'd yelled. No, I'm wrong about that. It was the entire audience. Even Jesse's mother, who stood on the stage in front of the choir with her back to the audience, looked over her shoulder at me. You'd think as choir director she would have been professional about the whole thing and gone on with the next song, but you would be wrong. She kept staring at me, waiting, I suppose, to see if I had any other announcements to share with the crowd.

"Well," Jesse said in a quiet voice, "I guess I'm ready to leave after all."

"I'll find my own way home." I stood up and stormed toward the door. The choir finally began their next number, but by that time it was too late. They'd lost the crowd's attention. Every single pair of eyes followed me across the room. Including Wilson's and Bridget's. She looked like she was waiting for me to get out of earshot so she could laugh, but Wilson, well, Wilson's wide eyes were harder to read. I had no idea what he thought.

"You did what?" Dante said after I'd told him what happened. He stood over motorcycle parts in our garage and shook his head like he hadn't understood me.

"I broke up with Jesse because he's working on Wilson's campaign instead of yours. I thought you should know." After all, everyone else did.

More head shaking on Dante's part. "Sheesh, Giovanna, it's a high school election, not a kidney transplant."

Okay, I hadn't expected him to give me a hug or anything, especially since his hands were all greasy. But still, I had expected a more touching response. Maybe a thank you.

"He's working against you, Dante. Friends aren't supposed to do that."

"He said he owed Wilson a favor. I could understand that. It just means I'm going to have a great time rubbing it in when Wilson loses."

I leaned against the door frame and folded my arms. "Why does Jesse owe Wilson a favor?"

Dante shrugged. "I don't know. They've been friends

for a long time. Wilson's probably done a lot of stuff for Jesse."

I resented my brother's calmness. My own insides hadn't stopped churning since I stormed out of the hotel ballroom. In a harsher voice than I should have used, I said, "Jesse told me he doesn't think you have a chance because you're a newcomer."

"Yeah, well, Jesse is wrong about a lot of things. For example, he rides a Buell motorcycle. Those things break down so often they ought to come standard with tow rope." Dante finally straightened up and looked at me. "You don't have to break up on my account. I don't care if you go out with him."

"Well, it's too late. I already announced it. Inadvertently. To the whole audience during a song break."

Dante shook his head again. "I told you that you were too emotional."

I could think of many problems I had right then, and none of them had to do with my emotions. They all had to do with guys who liked motorcycles.

After I went inside—slamming the door to prove to Dante I wasn't too emotional—I walked over to the phone to call one of my friends. I wished, not for the first time, that I had a twin sister instead of a brother. A sister would have understood how I felt instead of treating me like an idiot for being loyal. Plus, if I had an identical sister, she could, you know, pretend to be me until people forgot I'd humiliated myself at a library fund-raiser.

I picked up a cordless phone, headed to my room, and tried to decide which of my friends to call. I usually talked to Charity when I had a problem. She's one of those compassionate types of people who feeds stray animals, which is why—much to her parents' chagrin—her yard has turned into a cat sanctuary. Well, really, when you think about it, it was her parents' fault. What did they expect when they named their daughter Charity?

But I didn't dial her number. Charity's father is a minister, which means she's an expert on forgiveness and turning the other cheek and all that stuff I don't do very well. I knew she'd tell me to apologize to Jesse.

I also didn't call Raine. Her name is actually Loraine, but she will hurt you if you call her that. Raine always tries to look at things logically, which, let's face it, never works. Besides, she doesn't date much because she's six feet tall (five eleven and three quarters, she claims), and she refuses to go out with anyone shorter than she is. This doesn't leave many guys to choose from. So I didn't imagine she would have the most sympathetic ear about my love life.

I lay down on my bed and dialed Daphne's number. Her cell phone number, that is, since it was a Saturday night and she was probably out on a date. I hoped not an important date, or at least not a date where she couldn't talk to me.

She picked up after two rings. I could hear music playing in the background. "Hey Giovanna."

"Hi, Daphne. Where are you? Are you busy?"

"I'm at Allison's party," she yelled over the music. "What's up?"

I put one hand over my eyes, as though this would keep me from crying, and told her the whole story.

After I'd finished, she said, "I can't believe Jesse would campaign for Wilson instead of for you and Dante. And then he doesn't see why you're upset about it. Men are nothing but fools. Really." Of course this statement would have carried more weight if I hadn't heard her immediately afterward turn to someone at the party and say, "Can you be a darling and get me a Dr Pepper?" Then there was a pause in which I heard her giggling in top flirting fashion. "Thanks, Troy."

As far as I knew, Daphne wasn't going out with anyone named Troy, but she goes through guys quicker than most people go through gum, so I didn't bother asking who he was.

"I'm really sorry for you, Gi," she said, returning to our conversation. "Do you want to get together soon and hang out?"

"Maybe." I didn't know what I really expected her to say to make me feel better. She could have promised me that pony I had wanted since I was seven years old, and it wouldn't have helped.

"Just a second, Giovanna." Daphne's voice turned far away again. "Did someone bring donuts? Are there any maple kinds? I'd love you forever if you'd get me one." A pause in which she turned up the flirt. "Pleeeease, Jared." A giggle. "I'm yours forever."

Jared? What had happened to Troy, and why was it that Daphne could eat whatever she wanted and never gain a single pound? Life is so unfair.

"Sorry, Gi, I'm back now. Let's go shopping Monday after school. That way Charity and Raine can come too, and we can turn it into a campaign strategy shopping trip."

I let out a breath I hadn't realized I'd been holding. Since Jesse had abandoned Dante, I almost expected all of my friends to vote for Wilson too. "That would be nice," I said.

"I've gotta go now, all right?"

Sure. Fine. I appreciated how much work it must take to simultaneously flirt with two guys and send them on errands for you.

I hung up and tried to muster some confidence in Dante's chances. My friends would help me. We would figure out a way to help him win. We had to. Because that would show Jesse he'd been wrong all along.

I lay on my bed for a long time, wishing I could sleep. I told myself I wouldn't think about Jesse or Dante or any of it. But the thoughts stayed hovering at the corners of my mind. I'd remember how Jesse had caught up with me in the hotel lobby. "You can't walk home," he said. "I'll drive you." He hadn't said this in a nice way. It wasn't like he was sorry.

"I'll call Dante. He can pick me up."

"I'm driving you." Jesse took hold of my elbow and steered me outside. "It's not like I want to stick around here anymore."

I felt myself flush and was glad he didn't look at my face. I mean, what was it with me that every time I got angry, it somehow turned into a public event?

I got into his truck, because it seemed childish to keep protesting, but I sat stiffly on the seat with my arms folded and looked out the window. Neither of us spoke until we pulled onto my street. Then he said, "One day you'll understand why I did this."

"That's all you have to say?" I asked.

He nodded. "Until the election is over, there doesn't seem much point in saying anything else."

And then what? I was going to forget he'd chosen to be

loyal to Wilson instead of Dante and me? No wonder Jesse was friends with Wilson. Apparently they had the same arrogance level.

I tried to erase all memories of the evening. I pulled my covers tighter around me and thought of my shopping trip Monday with my friends. Daphne could pick out clothes to make anyone look like a model. She'd help me find something wonderful.

But it wouldn't be a prom dress. Jesse and I wouldn't go together now.

I took a deep breath and repeated, "It doesn't matter," over and over again in my mind.

I pressed my eyelids together, trying to force sleep into relieving me of my thoughts. It didn't help. The tears came, then turned into sobs, and I lay awake on my bed for a long time.

Chapter

5

Sunday passed in a blur. I spent most of the time hidden in my room doing homework. My emotions swung between fierce determination to win the election, and abject misery in losing Jesse. To tell the truth, it was mostly abject misery, but I didn't see how I could have done things differently. Despite Dante's calm objections that he didn't care, I knew he did, or at least that he would.

I couldn't be loyal to my brother and have Jesse. Family was more important.

Still, it was misery.

Jesse didn't call, which shouldn't have surprised me, but I sat tensely in my room waiting to hear his voice anyway.

My friends called to check up on me and offer their sympathy. Daphne told me there were other fish in the sea. Charity told me I needed to look for the silver lining in this cloud of heartbreak. And Raine told me it was good that I found out now where Jesse's loyalties lie and not after we'd been married and he kept leaving me to go hang out with his buddies while I was stuck at home with three screaming babies and a sink full of dirty dishes. Raine probably watches too much *Dr. Phil*.

Anyway, I knew they were trying to make me feel better, but I didn't. I guess that's impossible the day after a breakup. You can't just pick up and move on like it all meant nothing.

Charity and Raine both rearranged their schedules so they could meet Daphne and me at the mall on Monday. Charity had to find someone to babysit her younger brothers and sisters, and Raine got someone to cover her shift at the Bickham country golf resort. She cleans rooms at the hotel there.

This in itself was the kind of gift that makes you love your friends.

I planned on asking Dante if he wanted to come too, but when I mentioned at dinnertime that I wanted to go to the mall after school, Gabby calmly vetoed it.

"I need you and Dante to clean out the garage. I'm planning on having a garage sale next weekend."

"But we were going to have a campaign meeting there too—you know, to help Dante."

"At the mall?" Gabby's voice turned incredulous. "You

want to hang out with your friends and your boyfriend at the mall and call it a campaign meeting?" She shook her head like she couldn't believe I'd suggested it. "I need your help here. You can schedule a mall trip some other time."

I glanced at Dante. Apparently he hadn't told our parents that Jesse had switched loyalties, and I didn't feel strong enough or numb enough to do it now.

Dante had been talking with Dad while Gabby and I spoke, but he tuned in during Gabby's last comment. "A campaign meeting at the mall?" he asked. "Sorry, I don't want to trail your friends around and watch them shop."

"We wouldn't be shopping the entire time," I said.

Gabby leaned forward, her eyes glinting. "No one's going to the mall tomorrow. You're cleaning out the garage."

I didn't even try to appeal to my dad. I'd learned from experience that he doesn't concern himself with these types of parenting details. Whenever I ask him if I can go anywhere, he generally answers with something horrible, like, "Well if it's all right with Gabby, I don't mind."

So I let the subject drop. But the next day I told Dante I'd pay him to clean out my half of the garage after school, and I caught a ride with Daphne to the mall. I wasn't trying to be defiant, it just seemed like a practical solution, especially now when I wanted to be with people who cared about me. I needed it.

If I had told Gabby about my breakup with Jesse, she wouldn't have consoled me. She would have told me all the ways I had handled the situation wrong and then made me go clean out the garage. Besides, we'd be home before Gabby got off work, and she'd never be the wiser. But just in case, I turned off my cell phone.

When we arrived at the food court, Charity and Raine were already there waiting at a table by Panda Express. Charity looked behind me. "Is Dante coming?"

I shook my head. "He's caught in a Gabby work vortex, but we can brainstorm and then tell him what we came up with."

Raine picked up a pencil and hovered it over a notebook. "We went over a few campaign ideas while we waited for you to get here. Exactly how much do you plan on spending for posters, buttons, that sort of thing?"

I shrugged. "I don't know."

Raine tapped the pencil against her notebook. "You're the campaign manager, haven't you talked to Dante about it?"

"Not really," I said.

Raine let out a disgruntled sigh to let me know, I suppose, that I was a lousy campaign manager. "Wilson will spend a lot," she said. "He's got money and his family name to uphold. If Dante wants to compete, he'll need to put out some cash."

"Money isn't Dante's image," I said. "He's running against that sort of thing. His posters should show he's an everyday student."

"The everyday student who rides a motorcycle and wears a black leather jacket," Charity said.

Charity's parents won't let her ride on a motorcycle, because they think motorcycles are too dangerous and borderline rebellious. Dante once offered her a ride home and she had to refuse him.

This has caused Dante to give her no end of grief about the subject. When she's at our house, he refers to his bike as either "the death trap" or "the Demonmobile." Sometimes he lets out a possessed-sounding cackle and pretends he's trying to get her. At some point during her visits, she usually ends up hitting him.

"Giovanna's right," Daphne said. "Image is everything. If we want to win, we've got to use Dante's image to his advantage."

"You mean we'll try to appeal to everyone's sarcastic, cynical side?" Charity asked.

Raine leaned forward across the table toward her. "Wilson is popular, but a lot of people at school resent popularity. You know, the snobbery, the cliques—how they look down on the rest of us. We've got to use that to our advantage."

"Don't be ridiculous, Raine." Daphne twirled her pencil between her fingers. "No one at school looks down at you."

Raine let out a grunt like she thought Daphne was making fun of her height. "Yeah. No one looks down on me without a ladder, right?"

Daphne rolled her eyes. "Don't be so touchy. I just meant that no one looks down on any of us."

Daphne, I should say right now, is the most popular of my friends. She flits from social group to social group, defying the boundaries that keep the rest of us in place. We have never figured out how she does this. It may be that she seems to like everyone at school, or it may be because she's gorgeous and has mastered flirting so well she could list it as a skill on a job application.

Whatever it is, Daphne doesn't quite live in the real high school world, and mostly we're glad she still wants to hang with us, as opposed to, say, striking out for Hollywood.

"Let's get something to eat," Charity suggested, breaking the tension between Raine and Daphne, "and then we'll talk more about the elections."

We went in separate directions to order food, then congregated back at the table and threw out campaign slogans while we ate.

" 'Rise up against the ruling class, vote for Dante,' " Raine said.

" 'It's time for a party that can party,' " Daphne said.

Charity took a sip of her drink. " 'Vote Dante, he has better hair than Wilson.' "

We all stared at her.

"What?" she said. "It's the best presidential quality he has."

Did I mention Charity and Dante don't always get along?

We kept throwing ideas around, then Daphne came up with a phrase that really caught my attention. She said, "Oh, there's Jesse."

I had heard the term "my heart leapt" before, but I always thought it was one of those clichéd metaphors like "It's raining cats and dogs." I've seen a lot of storms, and not once have I seen a downpour of poodles. But the thing was, my heart actually leapt. I felt it jump inside my chest.

I looked up.

Jesse wasn't alone. Bridget walked beside him. The two strolled across the food court, talking to each other and laughing. Jesse had apparently not only picked up and moved on after our relationship, he'd dropped several IQ points as well.

What a jerk.

I stared at the two of them, unable to pull my gaze away.

"Whoa, he didn't waste any time, did he?" Raine said.

I gulped. It felt like I'd swallowed glass. I couldn't answer.

Jesse and Bridget passed near enough to our table that they couldn't help but notice us. He did a double take and she gave a little wave and went, "Howdy." Then she stood even closer to him and smiled at me. You know, a sort of I've-stolen-your-boyfriend smile.

Daphne looked up at the two. "Out shopping—or did you decide to join our meeting and campaign for Dante after all?"

Bridget tossed her hair off her shoulder with disdain. "Not likely."

"We're ordering some shirts at the T-shirt shack," Jesse said. "For Wilson's campaign."

"Then we're meeting some people and going to a movie," Bridget said. "You know, Wilson's friends." She cast a knowing glance at Jesse, but he was looking at me, not her, so he didn't catch it.

Daphne said, "Oh really, who?"

Bridget counted the names off on her fingers. "Luke, Stacey, Micah Barnes, Anjie Eller . . ." Which is what you'd expect. Micah was captain of the baseball team, and Anjie was captain of girls' basketball. Apparently Wilson was collecting captains to help him out.

While Bridget and Daphne made small talk about who

was and wasn't showing up at the mall, Jesse continued to stare at me. "So you're already having a campaign meeting?"

I forced my voice to sound upbeat, as though it didn't hurt to see him with Bridget. "I told you Dante was serious about running."

Jesse looked over my head and then at both sides of the food court. "Where is he then?"

"He had other things to do."

"Other things besides attending his own meeting?"

I shrugged, refusing to concede the point. "Where's Wilson?"

"He'll be here."

"Oh, right. You came early to order shirts." My gaze slid over to Bridget. "That's obviously a job that takes two people."

A smile spread across Jesse's face. He seemed entirely too happy about my jealousy, so I pointedly ignored the fact that he is gorgeous when he smiles.

Jesse took a step closer to me. "I figured when buying clothes, I'd best get a woman's opinion, and you wouldn't be likely to help me. But if you're having second thoughts about helping Dante . . ."

"I'm not." Out of the corner of my eye I could see Raine and Charity. They were pretending to be engrossed in Daphne's conversation with Bridget, but I knew they were listening to Jesse and me. I tried to sound confident. "I'm supporting my brother. He'll make a great president."

Jesse shot me a challenging grin. "It's not gonna happen."

"When Dante wins, you'll have to eat every word you just said."

"If he wins, I'll eat my boots."

I pointed a finger in his direction. "I'll hold you to that."

Jesse's blue eyes glinted. "And what will you do when Wilson wins?"

"Lose my faith in humanity."

He laughed and shook his head. "No, if I'm eating my boots when Dante wins, you've got to come up with something a little better when Wilson wins." He peered under the table at my feet. "What are those Reeboks made out of?"

"I'm not eating my shoes."

"You're not as sure about Dante winning when there's leather on the line, are you?"

And then I couldn't back down. "Fine. Whatever. I'll eat a pair of my shoes, but not the Reeboks. They were expensive."

Jesse's cell phone rang. He took it out of his pocket and glimpsed at the caller ID. "There's Dante now." He took a few steps away to take the call in private while I stared at my shoes and wondered if it would be lethal to eat a pair.

I mean, let's face it. There was a much greater chance that I'd be sawing up a pair of high heels than there was that Jesse would be chewing down chunks of his cowboy boots.

"Giovanna!" Jesse motioned me over to where he stood and pushed the mute button on his phone. "I thought it was Dante, but actually it's your stepmom." One of his eyebrows rose, and he tilted his head at me. "Do you have any idea why she would holler at me for being with you at the mall?"

"She's pretty much psychotic," I said.

"Could it be you didn't tell her you were coming here?"

"Well, that too."

He shook his head and handed me the phone.

I released the mute button and held the phone to my ear. "Hello?"

That's really all I got to say. The rest of the phone conversation was Gabby screaming at me because she'd come home early in order to supervise the garage cleanup, and I'd disobeyed her and gone off to the mall.

"Don't think there won't be consequences for running off with your boyfriend after I told you that you couldn't," she yelled. "It will be a long, long time before you go out with Jesse again!"

See, it pays off to keep your stepmother uninformed about your love life. As far as the punishments she could have dished out, that one wasn't too bad.

Over the next few days I immersed myself in the election. Technically, we couldn't start campaigning until after we'd gathered enough signatures to put our candidate's name on the ballot. The office wouldn't hand out petitions until next Monday, but that didn't stop Wilson from planning things anyway. I heard through the grapevine—which generally meant Daphne—that Wilson had bought his popularity cohorts some shirts which read "WILLsonPOWER." They were all going to wear them during the campaign. He'd also ordered buttons and pencils with this logo.

All this information panicked me, because I didn't know where or how to make up buttons or any of the other stuff. In my free time I worked on posters, so we'd have a few ready. I also tried to think of a campaign jingle—which you'd think Dante would appreciate, but instead he kept saying, "Don't you dare put my name into something that sounds like a laundry commercial."

Stephen and Brandon, two of Dante's rebel friends who only went to school when it didn't interfere with their other plans, agreed to help with the campaign. They came up with the slogan "Let's make election day Dante's Inferno." Which if you ask me (and obviously no one did even though I was supposed to be the campaign manager) didn't make any sense. Dante's *Inferno*? That was some medieval book describing the levels of hell, which hopefully would have very little to do with our school elections. I vetoed the idea, but Stephen and Brandon went off and made posters with that slogan on it anyway.

It's hard to be in charge of rebellious people, because they don't take direction well.

During school I spoke to everyone I could, trying to encourage them to join Team Dante. This was excruciatingly hard for me. Since the biology room break-in, I always worry that anyone who isn't my friend is telling Giovanna-kleptomaniac jokes behind my back. And yes, there are several.

"Knock knock." "Who's there?" "Giovanna, so you'd better hide your valuables."

And "What did Giovanna win when she entered a beauty pageant?" "Miss Demeanor." I'm pretty sure Bridget came up with that one.

Anyway, it was hard for me to go up to people and strike up conversations, but I did. Every time I talked to a cute guy, I had the vague hope that Jesse would round the corner, see me talking to some studly rival, and be wounded by jealousy. This never happened, although every time I rounded a corner I saw Bridget glued to his side.

You'd think with all the guys I talked to, one or two of them might have shown some interest in the newly single me. I mean, before I went out with Jesse, guys occasionally flirted with me, but not anymore. It was totally depressing.

During lunch on Thursday I brought up this subject with Daphne. "Is there something wrong with me?" I asked as I sat down at our table. I'd just been through the lunch line, where despite a lot of smiling on my part, the guys in line had shown as much interest in me as they might to a nun in full habit. "It's the biology break-in, isn't it? Nobody wants to take a criminal to prom."

Daphne let out a sigh and twirled the end of her straw in her mouth as though unsure whether to tell me a secret or not. "Actually, Jesse told all the guys he knows that they'd better not ask you out."

"What?" I looked around the lunchroom, searching for Jesse so I could, I don't know, pelt him with carrot sticks or something. "He can't do that. We're not dating anymore."

Daphne nodded sympathetically. "I know. It totally violates the rules of breakup procedure, but obviously he's not over you yet."

Raine bit into a chip. "Or he wants to make you suffer."

I ignored her. "He told guys not to date me? He actually had the nerve to do that while he and Bridget have been traipsing around the school like a pair of magnets?"

Charity watched me, her eyes turning sympathetic. "It sounds like the two of you need to sit down and talk things out."

I picked up my utensils and cut into my salad with more force than was necessary. "Yeah, the last time we talked things out I ended up in an agreement where I may have to eat my shoes."

Raine shrugged. "You could always start hitting on the freshmen. I bet Jesse didn't threaten any of them."

Daphne leaned across the table as though she had the answer and it was already settled. "You need to meet some guys from Swain Academy. I know tons of them. I can set you up." Daphne's flitting between social groups didn't stop at Bickham High's doors. She also frequented parties from Bickham's only other high school, Swain Academy.

I pushed a tomato chunk back and forth between two pieces of lettuce. "I don't know. Blind dates never work out."

"Who says?"

"Anyone who's ever been on a blind date before."

"That's because they've never been on one of my blind dates." Her eyes narrowed, considering me. She leaned back in her chair. "You're on the quiet side, so you need someone who's outgoing, someone who knows how to have fun." Her head tilted and she looked into my face with the intensity of a fortune-teller gazing at a crystal ball. "And yet you're half Italian, which means you'll need someone with an untamed, passionate side as well."

I didn't contradict her, even though the only thing really Italian about me is my name. I've never been to Italy and know approximately twelve words of the language— and all of those are curses I picked up from Grandma Petrizzo.

Daphne gave me a motherly smile. "And yet you're in a fragile state of mind, so he'll need to be gentle and understanding too."

With her elbow on the table, Charity rested her chin in her hand. "Does this guy really exist? Because if Giovanna doesn't want him, I do."

Raine nudged her. "You can't date until you're sixteen. I claim the leftovers."

"I'm almost sixteen," Charity said. "July isn't that far away."

Charity skipped a grade back in elementary school. The downside of being this smart is that when you reach your junior year, you still can't drive. Plus, Charity's parents have a no-dating-until-you're-sixteen rule. It's partially due to her religion, and partially because Charity's dad has counseled too many teenage boys over the years.

Also, if you're a petite blond with an angelic face, like Charity is, people tend to mistake you for a freshman and volunteer to show you where your classes are.

"So do you actually know a guy like this?" I asked Daphne. "You know, an outgoing, fun, passionate, understanding guy?"

"I know several," she said.

Which should have made me suspicious right then. I mean, there are probably only several outgoing, fun, passionate, understanding guys on the whole planet. What were the chances that Daphne knew all of them? But you know, a woman in the desert longs for water, and I'd been parched all week.

"I guess I wouldn't mind you setting me up then," I said.

"Are any of those guys over six feet?" Raine asked. "Because if they are, I think you should throw one my way."

"I can set you up too," Daphne said. She straightened up in her chair. "I can be a matchmaker to all of you, no problem. But first we've got to find a man for Giovanna." She smiled, obviously pleased with herself. "It shouldn't take too long. After all, Gi is loyal, kind, and gorgeous."

See, that statement should have been my second clue that Daphne wasn't the best one to set me up. I mean, the girl obviously hallucinates. I could believe "pretty" on my good days. You know, the ones where I actually have time to do my hair and makeup, as opposed to most mornings, when I simultaneously try to do my hair, apply mascara, and eat toast.

Still, instead of seeing any red flags, in my head I was all, "I'm gorgeous. Daphne says so, so it must be true. Daphne can find me a guy and solve all my problems."

As if finding a guy to solve your problems isn't a contradiction of terms.

Chapter

6

I'll skip a long, drawn-out account of the two dates that followed over the weekend, because frankly, that would be too painful, but I'll give you the highlights.

Date number one: Dave picked me up Friday night at Grandma Petrizzo's house. Grandma's house had become my dating headquarters, since I was grounded for three weeks, although technically I was only grounded from going out with Jesse, which I totally wasn't doing.

Still, I knew Gabby wouldn't see it that way, because anyone who grounds their daughter from seeing her boy-friend for three weeks, just because she went to the mall when she wasn't supposed to, is completely evil. So of course I didn't mention to my parents that I'd broken up with Jesse, and I made Dante promise not to tell them. Then I went to spend the weekend at Grandma's. Gabby couldn't veto that, since Dad always encourages Dante and me to spend time with Grandma.

In case I haven't said it before, Grandma is the reason we moved to Bickham, Texas. When Dad's company offered him a job transfer here, he took it, because Grandma is nearly eighty and should be near family. Grandma is getting "eccentric," as my father puts it. Gabby uses other, less flattering adjectives. Anyway, Gabby didn't want to leave California and thought if Grandma got too eccentric to live on her own, then we should put her in a nursing home. This, I can tell you, did not go over well with Grandma.

Out of the blue she will launch into speeches about how in the old country children take care of their parents. They show respect. They understand the sacrifices a parent makes for a child, and they don't forget.

Grandma could develop full-blown amnesia and I bet she'd take one look at Gabby, raise a finger in accusation, and say, "In the old country . . ."

So basically Grandma and I had bonded over our mutual dislike of Gabby, and Grandma was more than willing to help me subvert my punishment by letting me go out with guys while I stayed at her house.

While I put on my makeup, I told her I'd broken up with Jesse and so Daphne was setting me up. She nodded, mulling over this information, then said, "I know a nice young man from church—Gary Gunther. He's out of high school but still lives with his mother. Just down the street. Such a nice boy and always helping his mother. Mows her lawn every week. I sit by him at bingo. I bet he'd be interested in meeting a beautiful Italian girl."

"Out of high school? He sounds too old for me, Grandma."

Grandma waved a hand in the air. Half her language consists of hand waves. I'm really not sure she'd be able to talk at all if someone tied her arms down. "I'm not suggesting you date Methuselah. He's a young fellow. He still has all his hair." Grandma leaned in close to me to emphasize her next point. "And he's nice to his mother. You can always tell how a man will treat his wife by the way he treats his mother." Which of course was the perfect introduction to the "In the old country" speech.

The doorbell rang. "That's probably Dave," I told her, and I headed to the living room.

She followed after me, still talking. That's the thing about Grandma. She really misses having company around, and so when someone comes to visit, she gives them all her pent-up conversation whether they're listening or not. "Your mother, God rest her soul, would never have suggested a nursing home. Your mother, she was a saint. Not like this new wife. I told your father to find a nice Catholic girl, and the first time, he listened to me.

But the second time—*ai*—you see what comes from not listening to your mother."

I answered the door. A guy tall enough to make Raine happy stood on the doorstep. He was cute, not as cute as Jesse, but I suppose that would have been asking too much. One can only expect a guy to have so many good qualities, and I'd already chosen outgoing, fun, passionate, and understanding.

He grinned at me. "Howdy, I'm Dave."

"I'm Giovanna."

Grandma peered around my shoulder. "Are you Catholic?"

He smiled back at her. "Not during Lent. Then I'm Episcopalian."

"Episcopalian?" Both hands went up. "No good will come from it. Mark my words."

Grandma said more, but it was in Italian, so we couldn't make out the further pronouncements about our doomed relationship.

I'm not sure which embarrassed me more, that she didn't get his joke or that in the first twenty seconds of our meeting she'd managed to insult not only my date, but an entire religion as well.

So anyway, that was the good part of the date. From there it went downhill.

First of all, Dave drove ten miles under the speed limit

at all times. In the beginning I thought he was just a cautious driver, but so many cars passed us, cutting around us and then back into the lane, that I grabbed my armrest, waiting for someone to sideswipe us.

While he was telling me about his graduation plans, I was bracing for impact. After a couple of cars honked at us, he shook his head and said, "Some folks are in such a hurry."

"You like to take your time to get places?" I asked, wondering if this was a part of being outgoing, fun, or understanding.

"Have you seen the price of gas lately? You can save yourself five or ten dollars a week by driving slower."

Or maybe he was cheap.

In the end "cheap" proved to be Dave's overriding quality—just barely beating out "boring." We went to the dollar theater to see a movie, which I didn't mind since hey, I go there with my friends all the time, but he also sneaked prepackaged popcorn and soda cans underneath his jacket.

During the whole movie I was afraid someone from management would come and haul us both out of the theater for eating contraband snacks. Then after the movie as we got into his car he asked, "Do you want to get some ice cream?"

"Sure," I said. But this meant that he drove to a Circle

K, ran inside, and came back with two Fudgsicles. We ate them while sitting in his car in the parking lot.

It's not that I wanted him to spend a lot of money on me. I always feel guilty when guys do that. But come on, don't I at least rate a Dairy Queen drive-through?

I kept thinking that if Dave and I went to prom, he'd probably get the flower for my corsage off of someone's front lawn and want it back at the end of the night.

So yeah, Dave was strike one.

The next night a guy named Ronald took me out to dinner. I gave Grandma strict instructions not to mention religion, marriage, or how my date compared to the guy down the street. I'm not sure whether she followed my instructions, since she spoke nothing but Italian when he came to pick me up. She spoke a lot of that, though, in between hand waving and shaking her head in a disapproving manner.

Ronald had just moved to Bickham from Boston, and it took me a few minutes to adjust to his accent. Like, I stared at him blankly when he told me that his, "Ca was pocked by the yad." So then he stared back at me because I didn't walk over to his car, which was parked by the yard.

Well really, you couldn't blame me. I'd spent the last three years living in Texas, a place which puts a lot of effort into saying their R's.

We went to a nice place for dinner, but I only have a

vague recollection of it. You see, Ronald played on Swain's football team. I know this because he spent approximately nine tenths of our date telling me about his team, his coach, the plays he'd messed up, the plays he hadn't messed up, and the New England Patriots. I assume the Patriots are a football team. If Ronald took a brief conversational detour to discuss the American Revolution, I missed it because by that time I was running trig problems in my mind to keep my brain from exploding.

So that was basically my second date. After Ronald took me home, I sat in the living room and talked with Grandma, although mostly she did the talking, and I wondered if I would ever find someone who I liked as much as Jesse. You know, someone who could stop time just by looking at you.

Monday before school everyone on Dante's campaign got together in the library for a strategy meeting. And this time Dante joined us. While we waited for Charity to show up, Daphne and Raine pumped me for details about my weekend. I told them a little about each date, enough to let them know why neither had worked out, and then added, "Maybe it's me. I don't think I'm good at blind dates." I mean really, I bet no one would ever buy Daphne a Fudgsicle at the Circle K.

Daphne leaned across the table closer to us so Dante

and his friends wouldn't hear her. "Well, probably you should have tried to steer the conversation away from sports with Ronald. If you're too shy to speak up, then guys only talk about their interests, and let's face it, that's not going to be anything you want to hear. Next time go with some subject matter in mind."

"Next time?" I asked.

"I have another date set up for you on Friday." She gave an airy laugh and shrugged her long blond hair off one shoulder. "Nathan called and asked if I could go out. I'm busy, but I told him I had this darling friend who was available. You'll like Nathan. He's hunky."

I would have turned the date down, but Daphne had already volunteered me. Besides, the word "hunky" kept repeating in my head.

Hunky was good. Hunky gave me something to look forward to, and heaven knew I needed something to make it through another week of watching Bridget throw herself at Jesse.

Finally Charity showed up. She dropped her book bag on the ground by the table and sank into a chair. "Sorry I'm late."

"You're always late," Dante said.

"And I'm always sorry," she said.

He rolled his eyes and passed out signature sheets so

we could collect the one hundred signatures we needed to put his name on the ballot. As Daphne tucked her petition into her books, she said, "We ought to have a party for the people who sign for Dante. You know, sort of a thank-you party."

Dante agreed without hesitation. "Great idea. We'll hold it next Saturday night at my house. We should tell everyone to bring a friend too. You know, get as many people as we can to support me."

See, I'd have to ask permission before I announced something like that, but this was Dante. He could invite two hundred people over to our house for a party without getting in trouble at all.

So with fifteen minutes left before classes began, we all headed out to different parts of the school for signatures.

I walked to the school's main staircase. Amid the flow of people, Jesse and Bridget stood together, clipboards in hand, talking to passing students. I hadn't expected to see him, and for a moment the sight made my heart squeeze together in surprise.

I turned away before he noticed me staring at him. Any time our gazes connected he felt the need to say something obnoxious, like, "Hey, nice shoes. They look tasty."

I walked down the hallway, not really knowing where to go, then headed out the main doorway and onto the courtyard in front of the school. It was as good a place as any to bother people.

Ginger and Erin, two girls from my Spanish class, walked toward me. They were just the sort I was looking for. You know, the kind of girls who'd been overlooked by the popular kids their whole life.

"Ginger," I called. "Hey, can you guys come over here for a second?"

They ambled toward me, Ginger swinging her clarinet case, and Erin popping her gum.

"My brother Dante is running for school president next year, and I'm collecting signatures to put him on the ballot. Will you sign for me?"

Erin popped her gum a few more times. "I haven't given any thought to who I want to vote for yet."

"You don't have to vote for him. There's plenty of time to decide that. This is just to put him on the ballot." I held the paper and a pen out to her, but she didn't make a move to take the pen. "We're throwing a party next Saturday at seven thirty," I said, still stretching out my arm. "And everyone who signs is invited. You can bring a friend. It will be fun."

Both girls looked at me and giggled as though I'd said something funny. I smiled back at them anyway. "Come on, say you'll come."

"But then they'd miss my party."

I must have jumped six inches when I heard Wilson's voice behind me. I mean, you'd think one of the girls might have clued me in that he stood right behind me. But no, they were probably waiting to see if I'd do something truly mortifying like say, "Sign Dante's petition because everyone knows what a jerk Wilson is."

Which at the moment I almost wished I'd said. Instead, I dropped my pen, and the paper fluttered from my hand onto the ground. While I picked them up, Wilson moved in on the girls.

"You know, I'm having a party at the exact same time as Dante's, so it looks like you ladies will have to choose whether you want to hang out with Biker Boy or come to the mayor's house." He leaned in toward them, his smile going full blast. "The pool is heated, so bring your swimsuits." He held out his clipboard to the group. "Speaking of swimsuits, you've lost weight recently, haven't you? You look great."

Erin took the pen and clipboard, blushing, then signed Wilson's sheet. I hoped she choked on her gum.

I turned and walked back toward the school. I wasn't about to stick around here and let Wilson steal people from me. As I went toward the door, I heard the rest of their conversation.

"What time is your party?" Ginger asked.

Wilson laughed. "That depends—what time did Giovanna say her party was?"

"Seven thirty," Ginger said.

"Then seven thirty it is."

Chapter

7

*A*ll the rest of the day it was the same. Wilson had suddenly transformed into Bickham High's own personal Don Juan. Wherever girls congregated, he was there, shoveling on the flattery, and in love with everyone he looked at.

I couldn't get anyone of the female gender to even look at my petition. It was ridiculous. I mean, after all, this wasn't a modeling contest. We weren't voting on some sort of escort service. This was student body president. And besides, Dante was as hot as Wilson, only in a less footbally, more Italian way.

The girls of Bickham should have seen right through all of those "You look great. Did you change your hair?" comments. I mean, we're girls. Of course we've changed our hair. That's what we do.

By lunchtime, the latest gossip centered on who Wilson would take to prom. He hadn't asked anyone, but suddenly a lot of junior girls thought they should go dress shopping just in case.

I still managed to get fifteen signatures, but these consisted mostly of geeky freshman boys who seemed far too happy to be invited to a party at my house. Several of them asked for my phone number.

I hoped Dante appreciated what I was doing for him.

Raine got people from the track team to sign. Charity hit up people from her church, and Daphne—well, Daphne was able to garner an easy fifteen signatures from junior guys who all wanted to date her.

After school, while Dante and I riffled through the refrigerator for snacks, Dante ranted about Wilson's tactics. "He purposely set out to sabotage my party. The guy is a total—" He glanced at Skipper, who sat eating Cheez-Its at the table. "S.O.B."

"What does S.O.B. spell?" Skipper asked.

"Sob," I said. "It means to cry."

Skipper's eyebrows scrunched together like she still didn't understand, but she popped another Cheez-It into her mouth instead of asking more questions.

"You know who else is a sob?" Dante asked. "Jesse is a total sob. He invited the whole basketball team to Wilson's party. He invited the entire second period biology class. He even invited my friends. I'm glad you broke up with him."

I fingered the grapes in my hand, not hungry anymore since the subject of Jesse had come up. And to think he'd told me he was going to use good sportsmanship. If this was friendly campaigning, what exactly was Jesse's definition of the unfriendly variety?

Dante took a package of lunch meat out of the fridge and tossed it on the counter. "We've got to stop Wilson from ruining our party. Let's change the date of ours."

"How would we let everyone know our new time? We're not sure who's coming as it is. We invited a bunch of people and are only hoping some of them show up."

"Then we'll have a better party."

I popped a grape into my mouth. It was sour, of course. I ate it anyway. "Better than a heated swimming pool? Better than at the mayor's house? While we're passing out potato chips, Wilson will have his party professionally catered by some French chef named Jacques."

"Then we'll ruin Wilson's party somehow." Dante ripped open a lunch meat package, folded up a piece of ham, and ate it without the bread. "Do you know anyone from your days in detention who could take care of the job?"

"Take care of the job how?"

"I don't know. We could set fire to his lawn ornaments or something."

I let out a grunt and waved one of my grapes at Dante. "You might have forgotten this, but I've already spent more than enough time talking to policemen. If you'll remember, I'm on probation."

"I know, I know. I was kidding." His eyes got a far-off look, and his voice slowed. "Still, I like the idea of a few of those potted palms going up in smoke. I mean, if you put trees in little bowls on your lawn, you're just asking someone to torch them."

"Don't do it," I said. "You might want to apply for something someday—like, say, college or a job—and tree-torching would look bad on your police record."

This was something I unfortunately knew too much about.

Dante threw a couple of slices of ham on a piece of bread, then reached back into the fridge for the mustard. "Yeah, I guess you're right. I'd planned on being the family delinquent, but you've already taken that title." He spread the mustard on his bread slowly, his humor, even his sarcasm, suddenly gone. "But I still don't want to let Wilson get away with it. He's turned our party into a contest. It's like the voting isn't secret. Everyone has to choose this Saturday who they support."

I didn't answer for a moment, because Dante was right. Still, I felt the need to say something, to somehow make it all better.

Dante and I have been looking out for each other for a

long time. Mostly these days I feel like I'm looking out for him, but it didn't used to be that way. When Dante and I first started kindergarten, my parents had to make sure we went to the same class, because I refused to talk to the teacher. Dante had to speak for me for half the year.

I leaned against the countertop and surveyed my brother. "Just because they go to Wilson's party doesn't mean they'll vote for him. And maybe we can think of something—you know, something legal—to help our cause."

Dante slapped the top piece of bread on his sandwich. "Do you suppose Dad and Gabby would let me hire a band?"

"Have you even asked them yet if you can have the party?"

He shrugged, picked up his sandwich, and took a bite. "I'll get around to it."

"Don't you think you should do it soon?"

"I'm sure it will be soon." He took another bite, and then I guess because I kept staring at him, he added, "I have a system. I'm waiting to ask Gabby at a time when I know she won't turn me down."

"When is that?" I didn't believe such a thing was possible, but if it was, I wanted in on it too.

He ignored me and wandered toward the kitchen door. "We should get a head count of all the people who are coming, so we know how much food and stuff to buy. Ask around and see which of the people that you talked to will be here."

"Right," I said, but I dreaded the thought. I mean, what if no one came?

The next day at school as Charity and I walked to our first period class, Dante came up beside us. "Get this. Wilson is telling people if they sign my petition they can't come to his party. Two people came up to Brandon today and asked him to cross their names off my list."

Charity let out a gasp. "That's terrible."

"Plus, Stephen only got four names and he's out sick today. Or skipping, but anyway, I'm eight names short."

Right after he said this, we walked past a guy who lives down the street from us. "Hey, Gibbs," Dante called to him. "Can you sign my petition?"

The guy shrugged and frowned. "Sorry, I already signed Wilson's."

"That's okay," Dante said, but as soon as the guy was out of earshot, Dante swore. Charity swatted him. She's trying to break him of his swearing habit through the gentle persuasion of smacking him whenever he does it.

The muscles tensed in his jaw. "You think this is easy?" he asked her. "Here, you collect some more names." He held the paper toward her, but she didn't take it.

"Sorry, but I got most of my names by telling people that my daddy would ask them to speak in church if they didn't sign." She let out a sigh. "I can only threaten so many people."

Dante shook his head. "My dad's an accountant. I have no leverage."

We continued to walk through the flow of students. Dante rolled up the petition and tapped it against his leg as his gaze darted back and forth through the hallway. He looked like he wanted to club someone with it.

Charity kept glancing at him. She shrugged and said, "Well, you could always act like Wilson and shamelessly flirt with some girls."

"Right," he said.

"Come on, let's see you strut your stuff. Put some of that Italian charm to good use." Charity pointed to a group of three girls standing by a locker. "There's some sweet young things, go convince them that you're the man they want."

Dante tilted his head at her but kept walking away from the girls. "Does your father know you talk this way when he's not around?"

She smirked at him. "Coward."

I tried to stop their argument by holding out my hand to Dante. "Give me the list. I'll get some names."

Dante shoved the list in my direction without looking

at me. His eyes narrowed as he considered Charity. "I can't believe you, of all people, would tell me to use people like Wilson does."

She tilted her chin downward and gave him a crooked smile. "Oh, give me a break. I knew you wouldn't do it. You don't know how to be charming."

His head jerked back as though she'd smacked him again. "What's that supposed to mean?"

She rolled her eyes.

I raised my voice. "So when I get eight more names—do you want the petition back during school so you can take it to the office, or should I bring it home?"

Dante still didn't look at me. "I know how to be charming."

Charity laughed, like it was funny.

"You want charming? I'll show you charming." He took the list from my hand and walked over to the drinking fountain where a couple of girls stood talking. They looked like easy enough targets. Freshmen. Maybe sophomores, but you could tell by the way they dressed that they wanted to be older. Well, either that or the expiration on their makeup was tomorrow and they were trying to use it all before it went bad.

I didn't want to stop. My trig teacher gets into a snit if we walk into class after the bell rings, but how could I keep from watching? Besides, Charity had firmly stopped. She leaned up against a locker with no apparent sign of ever moving again.

We watched as Dante smiled at the girls, leaned toward them, and laughed at something one of them said. Which was weird to see, because hey, this was my brother. It's hard to think of brothers as having a romantic side, since to us sisters, they are simply half-disgusting creatures who leave their dirty socks lying around, snore on the couch, and never clean the bathroom.

The girls laughed back at whatever Dante had said. One of them tilted her head and looked shyly up at him.

He handed her the paper and a pen. I could imagine him saying, "Have you lost weight lately? Have you changed your hair?"

How gross. "If he starts acting like Wilson now," I told Charity, "I will hold you personally responsible."

She let out a huff and sent an angry glare in Dante's direction, which was totally uncalled for, since she'd been the one to call him charmless in the first place. And then it hit me. Charity liked Dante. Why else would it tick her off that he was over there flirting with those girls?

Every memory I had of Charity and Dante together suddenly shifted. Things that had never made sense before became clear. I leaned against the locker next to her. "You know, next time you should be more specific and tell him who he's supposed to be using his charm on."

One of the girls took the pen from Dante's hand and wrote something on the paper. Charity tore her gaze from them. "What do you mean?"

"Tell him he's supposed to be charming you."

Her eyes widened, and then she let out another huff. "Why would I want that?"

Maybe I'd been wrong. "Never mind," I said.

She blinked, as though trying to erase any emotion from her large blue eyes. "It would never work out between us. I'm not sixteen yet. Besides, he rides a motorcycle. And he likes it."

Nope, I wasn't wrong. I smiled even though she looked cross and miserable. Half the time the girls Dante brought home were total idiots. Like in their zest for body piercing they got carried away and accidentally pierced a few necessary parts of their brains. Charity would be good for him. "Motorcycles aren't so bad. Well, you know, if you never look down."

Dante walked back to us with an extra bounce in his step. He smiled, folded a ripped piece of notebook paper, and slipped it into his jeans pocket.

"Did you get her signature for your petition?" Charity asked.

He handed the list back to me. "Nope. She'd already signed Wilson's, but she did give me her phone number."

Charity shook her head and walked toward class again.

I glared at Dante for her. I mean really, why would he want an underclassman who applied her makeup so it looked like she was testing paint swatches on her eyelids?

Guys. I turned my back on Dante and walked down the hallway with Charity.

"Arrivederci ragazze!" he called after us and then laughed.

I didn't try to get any signatures in trig class, because I barely made it through the door as the bell rang. This caused Mr. Ragolski's snit level to rise by several degrees, and I knew I'd get in trouble if he caught me passing the petition around.

Still, I needed to come up with eight signatures for my brother—and this because I had tried to keep Dante and Charity from fighting, which goes to show you that I should mind my own business or I should try to set them up.

I wasn't sure which.

After lunch I went to Honors English. It used to be my favorite class, because reading doesn't seem like homework to me. It's more like entertainment. Well, except for Hemingway, which could be used to hypnotize lab rats into semi-conscious states.

Unfortunately, Jesse is in my English class. So is Wilson. I'd been doing my best to avoid talking to Jesse in class, except for those times when he and Wilson were loudly discussing whether I was going to eat sandal-wiches or meatloafers.

Sometimes it felt like we hadn't broken up at all, and this teasing was the same kind of flirting we used to do. At other times I wanted to grab Jesse's boots and give him a head start on eating them.

As I walked to my seat, I glanced at Jesse. He sits two rows over from me. My gaze lingered on his broad shoulders, his jawline, the curve of his lips. I wondered if he'd already asked Bridget to prom. I wondered if he'd ever kissed her. Daphne probably knew the answer to these questions, but I didn't have the heart to ask her.

Mrs. Pembroke stood by her desk talking to a couple of students. She waved one hand around explaining something. I couldn't tell what, but judging from her motions it may have had something to do with directing an orchestra or guiding a plane safely onto a tarmac.

Mrs. Pembroke is a good teacher. Whenever we discuss books, she always takes our thoughts and opinions seriously. How many teachers do that? Most have their own opinions, and the whole point of class is for them to tell you their opinion and then grade you on it.

Of course, part of Mrs. Pembroke's attitude comes from the fact that she wants to be a writer and so is looking for reader feedback. She always asks us what we liked and disliked about a story. What was our favorite part? How would we improve the plot if we could?

We're sort of like a room full of teenage consultants.

Wilson, I noticed, was busy talking to a girl in the back of the room. No doubt campaigning. I decided to be a politician myself and scooted closer to the guy who sat in the row between Jesse and me. "Hi, Bill."

"Howdy." He glanced at me, then returned his attention to a paper he was writing.

Bill is a nice guy, despite the fact that he'd done a lot of eye rolling whenever Jesse and I had leaned over his desk to talk to each other. Really, he was probably relieved that Jesse and I had broken up so he didn't have to be in the middle of us anymore. I smiled at him anyway. "Have you signed anyone's petition for student body president yet?"

"No. Why? Are you running?"

This, I noticed, turned Jesse's head. I pretended not to see him. Instead I gave Bill my most lilting laugh. "No, not me. To tell you the truth, I wouldn't have the courage to run against Wilson. With his popularity, money, and connections—well, hardly anyone else stands a chance. But my brother, Dante, really wants to see things change. He's tired of the same old clique running the school. Would you like to help us by signing—"

I didn't get to finish. Jesse leaned on the other side of

Bill's desk. "A clique doesn't run the school. Student council does."

"It's the popular clique," I said. "Every day you can sit and watch them all cliquing away—"

Jesse cut me off. "They put in their own time, working hard to plan dances and fund-raisers—"

"But not memorials. They do whatever they want, and they couldn't care less about the rest of us." I put the petition on Bill's desk. "We can send a message to the elitists at this school by voting for Dante."

Jesse let out a grunt. "Elitists? You think Wilson is an elitist?"

"If the Prada shoewear fits, then yeah, he should wear it."

Bill looked at the petition, then glanced at the back of the room, where Wilson and his latest conquest were laughing at something. He gulped and didn't sign. "I . . . uh, think Wilson and Dante are both great guys," he said.

Jesse's eyes narrowed at me. "I suppose you think I'm an elitist too."

"Well, I didn't until you totally blew off Dante."

"I didn't blow off Dante. I started campaigning for Wilson."

"You invited Dante's friends to Wilson's party."

Jesse tossed up both his hands like I was the one being unreasonable. "I invited everyone I know. That's not being elitist, that's being inclusive. Besides, Dante can invite my friends to his party. I don't care."

And I could tell he didn't. His face registered only disbelief at my frustration. This was his idea of good sportsmanship? "Dante might have been able to invite your friends if Wilson hadn't planned his party at the exact same time Dante was throwing his party. Are you going to defend Wilson about that too?"

Jesse shrugged. "That's just normal politics. It's like contact sports. When you play football, you gotta expect you're going to be tackled a few times."

That was it? That was how he justified everything? Because it was okay to slam people to the ground in football?

He must have seen the incredulity on my face, because he tried to explain further. "Guys will fight to the death during a game, but after it's over, we're all friends again."

Men and their sports tactics. If he could claim that sort of thing as fair play, then I could just as easily pull out a few feminine wiles to help my cause. I shoved the petition closer to Bill and smiled at him, trying to muster as much charm as I could. I softened my voice and tilted my head so my hair cascaded off one shoulder. "I'd really appreciate your support."

Jesse frowned at me. He knew what I was up to. "Maybe Bill wants to keep his support to himself."

"I . . . um . . ." Bill said.

I cast a glare at Jesse. "Is this another one of your attempts to scare guys away from me?"

Jesse leaned back in his seat. "Not at all. If I was trying to scare him away from you, I would have said something like, 'Hey Bill, don't talk to Giovanna, and if you ever ask her out I'll make your life never-ending misery.'" Jesse smiled over at me. "And I clearly never said that."

I don't understand men. I mean, it would be one thing if Jesse was trying to make amends and win me back or something. But he hadn't done that. He'd never called or tried to talk to me. It was like this was all a game to him. I'd dumped him in front of everybody, so he was getting back at me by doing everything he could to ensure no one else asked me out.

I gave my pencil to Bill even though he already had one sitting on his desk. "Don't let him intimidate you. He's just one of the elitists whose rule is about to end."

Jesse looked at the ceiling and shook his head. "Come on, Gi. You can't call me an elitist. How many elitists do you know who wear cowboy boots and drive a motorcycle?"

"One," I said.

Bill pulled the petition toward him. "Here. I'll sign. No need for more discussion." His hand scurried across the paper. "I'm signing it."

Jesse shook his head at me again. "If you think my friends are elitists, you don't know them very well."

I kept my voice light, refusing to let any bitterness seep through. "Well, that might be true. After all, none of them ever spoke to me, so it was hard to get to know them."

Bill put both his hands down on his desk and let out a sigh. He glanced first at Jesse, then me. "And I thought you two were bad when you were dating. I'm never going to have a minute's peace in this class. I nearly took World History this period, but no, everyone said to pass the English AP test I needed Honors Lit."

I took my pencil and the petition from Bill's desk. "That reminds me, Bill. You're invited to a party at my house. This Saturday at seven thirty. You can bring a friend if you want."

Bill looked at me like I was crazy, which I supposed meant I wouldn't have to add him to the party head count.

Luckily, I didn't have to say anything else, because Mrs. Pembroke strode in front of the room. "Settle down, class. It's time to get started, but first I wanted to read something to you."

I turned around in my desk and looked at her. I held my pencil to my notebook paper in case I had to take notes, but I pressed down so hard the lead snapped off. Which is probably a sign that your ex-boyfriend has stressed you out.

Mrs. Pembroke read to the class from a piece of paper she held, which turned out to be her latest rejection letter for a mystery novel she'd written. My mind wouldn't focus on her words though. It was still back on the election. "Dear Ms. Pembroke," she read, "thank you for submitting your manuscript for our consideration . . ."

How could we win when we were struggling just to get Dante's name on the ballot? I felt tears threatening to appear, which is really not something you want to happen at the beginning of English, especially when your ex-boyfriend is sitting two rows over.

"We regret to inform you that your story does not fit our current publishing needs . . ."

Wilson was impossible to beat. Why was I even trying?

"We wish you the best in your publishing endeavors . . ."

The party on Saturday would be a flop, and Dante would be so hurt. A lot of times you go through life thinking you have friends and people like you. Maybe those assumptions should never be put to the test.

And then Mrs. Pembroke's words cut through my thoughts. She shook the piece of paper she held in her hand. "Sometimes I feel like quitting, but I'm not going to. What kind of teacher would I be if I taught you to quit just because you received a rejection letter or two—or in my case twenty-eight, but who's counting?" She forced a laugh and picked up the stapler from off her desk. "Do you know what I'm going to do instead? I'm taking all of my rejection letters and putting them on the classroom bulletin board. Then every time we see them it will remind us that it takes hard work and a lot of revision to get what you want in life."

She strode to the bulletin board, stapled the letter in the middle, then turned around and smiled at us. "Because I know that one day I'll staple an acceptance letter right up here."

Sometimes I wondered about the sanity of my teachers, and I have to say that this was one of those times. I mean, the woman had smiled at her rejection letter. That couldn't be normal.

Then she looked at me. "We should never give up."

For a moment I didn't breathe. Somehow Mrs. Pembroke not only knew about the election, but she'd read my mind and understood how I wanted to quit. All this was a message to me, telling me to believe in Dante's chances, and even to believe in the Bickham High student body.

Then her gaze moved on, and I knew I had imagined it all. Still, I tucked the petition into my notebook, more determined than ever to get our last seven names.

Before school ended I must have asked every single person in my classes to sign Dante's petition. Which is really saying something, since the last thing I wanted to do was get sent to detention again. By the time the last bell rang, I'd done it. Which ought to show Jesse—I mean, Wilson—something.

Although, to tell you the truth, I'm not sure how much Wilson actually paid attention. He flirted with Lorrel Stock—head of the swim team—through English, switched to Leslie Hanchet—tennis star—during Spanish class, and I saw him walking out of the school with Katheryne Blair—captain of the volleyball team. I guess you could say Wilson was well rounded when it came to sports.

I rode home from school with Dante. I used to ride home with Jesse, which is sort of the same, motorcycle-wise, but not at all the same otherwise.

Right after Dante dropped me off, he went to pick up Skipper from the babysitter's. She has morning kindergarten, then stays with a lady a few streets over until Dante and I get home from school. He walks, by the way. Skipper's not allowed anywhere near a motorcycle. We watch her (which usually means I watch her) until Gabby and Dad get home from work.

While I rummaged through the fridge looking for something to eat, the doorbell rang. I answered it without thinking. Jesse stood on my doorstep.

Chapter

8

At first I couldn't breathe. Then I couldn't speak. I just stood there looking at him. Had he always been so tall? Had his jaw been so perfectly square before?

He shifted a toolbox that he held from one hand to the other. "Is Dante home?"

"Oh. Um. No. He's picking up Skipper, but he'll be home any minute."

"I have some tools to return to him."

He held out the box to me, but I didn't take it. "Did you want to wait for him to come back?"

I thought Jesse wouldn't stay and face Dante, but he stepped inside. "Sure. I probably should talk to him about the ape hangers."

"The what?"

"The handlebars."

Apes, hogs. I never understood what he was talking about when he lapsed into motorcycle lingo.

Jesse walked to the living room, put the toolbox on the floor, then sat down on the couch. He knew the inside of my house as well as I did, and probably the nooks and crannies of the garage better. That's where he and Dante worked on their bikes.

I sat on the love seat, crossed my legs, and ran my fingers through my hair in what I hoped was a casual, I'm-over-you manner.

Jesse leaned back on the couch, putting one foot on his knee. He wore his cowboy boots, and I traced the design with my eyes.

"So . . ." He let the word drift off awkwardly, a poor opening for any conversation, then examined my face. "Are you still upset about English class?"

The question wasn't what I expected. I had already prepared myself for something generic, maybe a comment on the weather, and I blinked at him unspeaking.

"I'm not trying to be your enemy," he said.

Well, he had a funny way of showing it, but I decided to avoid another fight. I wouldn't be the stereotypical shrill, accusing ex-girlfriend. I would show him I was above such things. I put on a smile. "It's fine. I'm not upset."

He nodded, but I could tell he didn't believe me.

"I've moved on." I tried to make the words light and

aloof, but his nod took on an amused tilt. Did he really think he was so hard to get over?

"Well, I'm glad you're not mad at me." He forced a grin to disappear. "So what have you been up to lately?"

"The campaign takes a lot of time, and last weekend Daphne set me up with two of her guy friends—not at the same time, of course. I mean I went out with one on Friday and one on Saturday."

He raised an eyebrow. "Dante said you went to your grandmother's to spend time with her."

"I did. I spent time with her while I wasn't out on one of my dates."

"Oh." More suspicious nodding on his part. Which ticked me off, because—really, did he not think I was hot enough to rate two dates in one weekend? Okay, so they were blind dates with guys who had probably only consented to go out with me because they thought it would win them brownie points with Daphne, but that's beside the point.

"What have you been up to?" I asked.

He shrugged his awesomely broad shoulders in an obvious attempt to make it hard for me to breathe. And I admit my lungs had one quick spasm, but after that I was able to manage a disinterested expression.

He said, "I've been working with Wilson and his friends. You know, Luke, Stacey . . . Bridget."

"Yeah, I've seen you working with Bridget. She's about as subtle as Wilson."

Another quick smile on his part. "What's that supposed to mean?"

He knew what it meant, so I decided to ignore the subject of Bridget altogether. "Every time I turn around, Wilson has a different girl attached to his side."

Jesse laughed, and his voice grew soft. "I think that says more about the girls at our school than it does about Wilson."

Yeah, it said they were stupid.

I smiled back at him. "Well, I'm glad you're happy with your campaigning decision."

His gaze locked with mine, and his aqua blue eyes grew intense. "I will be."

The front door opened. I expected Dante, but instead Gabby walked inside. She opened the coat closet with one hand and put her briefcase inside with the other, then she turned back to us and sent a glare in Jesse's direction. "Jesse. I thought I recognized your bike out front."

"I came over to return some tools to Dante," he said.

Gabby's gaze swept across the living room. "Then where is Dante?"

"He's not back with Skipper yet," I said. "That's why Jesse is waiting for him."

Gabby twisted her lips into a disbelieving grimace. "How convenient. I come home early and find you here alone with your boyfriend. You just don't think rules apply to you."

I blushed. I hated her, but I didn't say another word.

She put one hand on her hip. "We'll discuss this when your father gets home. For now"—she turned to Jesse and let out a disappointed sigh—"you'd better go on home. And please don't come over to see Giovanna again until she's through being grounded."

Jesse opened his mouth but didn't speak. He glanced at me, I guess to see my reaction. Maybe he was surprised I didn't correct Gabby about his being my boyfriend. To admit that, however, was to let Gabby know she'd grounded me for three weeks for nothing.

Jesse stood up and said a quiet "Yes, ma'am," to Gabby. Then he looked from the toolbox to me. "So you'll tell Dante I came by?"

I nodded and stood up to walk him to the door, but just then Dante and Skipper came inside. Skipper let out a squeal of joy and, with her arms up, rushed to Gabby. "Mommy's home!"

Gabby gave her a quick hug, then set her back down. "Yes, Mommy is home early today, and it's a good thing too, because apparently I needed to be here." She shot me another one of her We'll-discuss-this-later looks, then turned and walked to the kitchen, shaking her head as she went.

Jesse nodded in Dante's direction. "I just stopped by to return your tools."

"Oh." Dante glanced at the toolbox. "Thanks." Then nothing more. An awkward silence filled the room.

Skipper stared up at Jesse with her head tilted. Her pigtails looked like crooked antennae. "You don't look like you've been crying."

"What?" he asked.

"Dante said you were a sob."

Immediately, Dante scooped up Skipper and flung her over one shoulder. "Let's go find Mommy."

Dante gave Jesse a hurried, "See ya," then headed to the kitchen, calling, "Hey Mom, can I talk to you for a sec?"

Jesse watched them go, then folded his arms. "So what was that all about?"

"I have no idea."

"Dante called me an S.O.B., didn't he?"

I didn't want to look at Jesse but found myself meeting his eyes anyway. "You can't blame him. You and Wilson are trying to ruin his party."

Jesse let out a sigh and walked to the door. "I'm going to be so glad when this election is over and things go back to normal."

As if they would.

Jesse put his hand on the doorknob, then paused and turned back to me. "Do you want me to talk to Gabby for you? You know, explain to her that I really did come by to see Dante."

"She wouldn't believe you," I said.

He paused for another moment. I waited for him to ask me why I hadn't told Gabby about our breakup, but instead he said, "Ironic that she's mad at you for this afternoon and not for going out with two different guys last weekend."

"What she doesn't know won't hurt me."

He leaned against the doorway. His eyes took on a mischievous glint. "I could tell her."

"You wouldn't dare."

He looked upward, as though considering the situation. "It would keep you from going out again. And even though you broke up with me, I just might be the jealous type who can't get over you."

"Yeah, I could tell that by the way you never take your eyes off of Bridget at school."

He smiled. "We're not talking about Bridget."

"I mentioned her name. You mentioned her name. That means we're talking about her."

His gaze moved to mine, and his voice dropped to a soft murmur. "I could blackmail you, you know. Something along the lines of you doing my bidding or I tell your stepmom everything."

I smiled back to show him I wasn't afraid. "Don't even think about it."

"How can I help thinking about it? There are so many things I could bid you to do." He rubbed his hand against his chin, still considering me with teasing eyes. "I have a vivid imagination, you know."

Yeah, I bet. He'd probably make me campaign for Wilson.

Jesse took a step toward me, his gaze intense. I caught the scent of his cologne. It was suddenly hard to breathe.

He was doing this on purpose—making me want to throw my arms around him, even though we were rivals now. It must have seemed funny to him, how easily he could maneuver my emotions. Perhaps he was taking girl-melting lessons from Wilson.

I moved closer to the door. "You need to go. If Gabby comes out and finds you here, she'll yell at me again."

He didn't budge. The teasing left his expression, but the intensity remained. "Promise me you won't go out again while you're grounded."

Why? I stared at him, trying to figure it out. I mean, despite this episode of flirting, I knew he didn't want me back. You don't ignore someone for eleven days—and yes, I'd been counting—if you wanted a reconciliation. You didn't tote around Bridget like she was some sort of fashion accessory if you had second thoughts.

I tried to read his intentions from his eyes. "Why do you care whether I obey Gabby or not?"

He gave me a crooked smile. "Blackmailers never explain their thinking. They're like pirates that way. Dark-hearted, dangerous—and cool like Johnny Depp."

I was not about to admit to him that he was right about that last part. Instead I peered over at the kitchen door. "If you don't go, you're going to get me in more trouble."

"All the more reason for you to agree to my terms."

"I can't. I already have plans for next weekend."

One of Jesse's eyebrows shot up. "Besides Dante's party?"

"Yes. I have another date with a guy from Swain."

He held one hand up, then dropped it in frustration. "You're out of control, Giovanna. You didn't go out this much when we were dating. I really should tell Gabby."

I didn't answer him. I folded my arms, and the two of us stood staring at each other in the doorway. "I'm going to tell her," he said. "One last chance to do my bidding."

I waited and didn't speak.

We stood there for another moment, then he let out a sigh and shook his head. "All right. You know me too well. I'm not dark-hearted or dangerous, and I guess I don't have it in me to blackmail you." He walked out the door, but then turned back around while he was still on the front step. "Don't let Daphne set you up too much, though. You know her judgment isn't the best."

This from the guy who was friends with Wilson and his minions of popularity. "What do you mean by that?"

"Remember that concert in Houston? She convinced the rest of you she could drive there. What part of the boondocks did you all end up at?"

I refused to concede the point. "Anyone can take a wrong turn off the freeway."

"How about that time she wanted to form a band?"

"It's not Daphne's fault the rest of us can't sing. The police probably wouldn't have kicked us off that street corner if we'd had better rhythm."

"Right. So don't trust her judgment, or who knows what will happen." He turned away from me and walked out to his motorcycle.

I shut the door, but somehow I couldn't pull myself away from the window until his bike had turned the corner.

When I finally walked into the kitchen, Dante sat alone at the table, popping Fritos into his mouth. He smiled when he saw me. "Gabby okayed the party."

I had known he had wanted something from her when he called her "Mom." She always transforms into "Mom" when Dante is about to ask her for something.

I pulled a glass from the cupboard and filled it with water. "I thought you were going to wait until she was in a good mood to ask her about the party. What happened to all of that I'll-ask-her-when-the-time-is-right stuff?"

He flipped another Frito into his mouth. "The time was right. When she's angry with you, she always bends over backward to be nice to me. It's like she has to prove to herself that she really is a good parent even though she comes down so hard on you." He held both his hands out. "I'm happy to oblige her."

I had taken a drink as he explained this, and now I nearly choked on it. I coughed and held my throat, trying to breathe. "You . . . you've been using my problems for your own advantage?"

He shrugged. "Someone should get some benefit out of Gabby's tirades."

I waved my hand in the direction of the living room. "I got in trouble because Jesse came to see you. You could have stood up for me. You could have told her she was wrong."

"But then we wouldn't be having a party on Saturday."

I slammed my glass down on the counter so hard that half the water splashed over the edges. "That's it, I quit, Dante. Find yourself another campaign manager. In fact, I'm voting for Wilson, because at least the people he uses are just miscellaneous groupies and not his twin sister."

Dante sighed and rolled his eyes. "There you go, getting all emotional again." He probably said more. I didn't hear it, because before he'd finished, I was halfway to my room.

I did my homework for the next few hours, and only emerged from my room long enough to e-mail Charity the message: "Dante's a jerk. You're better off without him."

Then I went back to my room.

My dad came in after he got home from work. He stood by the door, not looking angry, just old and tired. "It's almost time for dinner."

"I'm not hungry," I said.

"Gabby tells me she came home and found you with Jesse."

"Yeah," I said.

"Dante says Jesse came over to return some tools and was only here because he was waiting for Dante to come home. Is that right?"

"Pretty much."

Dad sighed, and I wondered if he was disappointed I was innocent. Maybe it would be easier if I was guilty so he could dish out whatever punishment Gabby wanted instead of having to defend me to her. He turned and put his hand on the doorknob. "Are you coming down to dinner?"

"No."

"All right." He opened the door and walked out of the room. Well, I shouldn't have expected more from him. I tried to turn my attention back to my Spanish homework but ended up looking at my bedspread instead. It's a pink checkered quilt that I've had for as long as I can remember.

When we were little and shared a room, Dante used to have a matching blue quilt. Every once in a while we would pull all the kitchen chairs in a circle and make a huge tent with our blankets. Inside became a secret, protected place, invisible to the world. At least until Mom peeked in and asked if anyone had seen her missing twins. Sometimes we'd come out, but sometimes she'd let us eat peanut butter sandwiches inside.

I know I wasn't always happy back then, but it seems that way now. My memories of that time are peppered with images of my mother smiling and Dante holding my hand as we climbed on the bus for kindergarten.

I lay down on my bed, listening to the sounds of dinner coming from the kitchen, and tried to soak up all the memories from my quilt.

So Dante had told my father the truth. I was still mad at him. At least for the moment. I never stayed mad at Dante for long. He'd spoken for me, back when I couldn't find my voice. But that wasn't why I forgave him. I forgave him because I knew what no one else did. When our mother lost her battle with cancer, a part of Dante's voice died with her. A part of him no longer spoke. I knew it, had sensed it happen, and I'd been trying to speak for him ever since.

That's why I wanted him to win the stupid election. It wasn't about Wilson or Jesse or any footwear I might have to choke down. Dante cared about something. He wanted to create a memorial for a friend. He was trying to do something good for someone else, and that was a part of him that had remained silent for far too long.

The noises of dinner stopped, and then I heard the clank of the dishes going in the dishwasher. I wondered who did them. Maybe Gabby had made Dante clean the kitchen, since he'd supported my version of the Jesse story.

Finally the noises stopped, and then someone knocked on my door. I didn't want to speak to anyone in my family, but curiosity got the best of me. "Come in," I called.

Dante opened the door and walked in with a plate of lasagna and garlic bread. He put it in front of me along with a fork and a knife, then sat down on the end of my bed.

It smelled warm and delicious. I have no pride where lasagna is concerned. I picked up the fork and took a bite.

He watched me for a few moments, then said, "You'll have to sneak the dirty dishes back downstairs when Gabby isn't around, or she'll go ballistic at you for eating out of the kitchen."

Like he had to tell me that. I took another bite and glared at him. "Wouldn't that make you happy? Maybe she'd finally buy you that big-screen TV you've always wanted."

He pulled one knee up onto my bed and leaned against my wall. "Has anyone ever told you that you're too emotional? Oh yeah—I have, on a daily basis."

I took another bite. "I can't believe you used my problems as a springboard for getting what you want. I mean, it's . . ." I set my fork down on my plate with a clang. "They let you buy your motorcycle right after I got in trouble for breaking into the biology room."

"Yeah, and if you ever decide to go on another crime wave, give me some advance notice. I'd like to prep Gabby for a sports car."

I came close to throwing my lasagna at him. The only thing that stopped me was knowing I'd have to clean tomato sauce off my carpet. And of course Gabby would find out about it, and then Dante would be halfway to winning a trip to Cancún or something.

"You are such a jerk," I said.

"There you go, getting all emotional again. I've been telling you forever that you handle Gabby wrong. You want some pointers?"

Well, not pointers exactly, but I did want something pointy to throw at him. I didn't say anything but did try to send him some hostile psychic twin messages while I ate.

"If you want to get on Gabby's good side, you've got to let her be your mother. She tries, but you cut her out of your life every opportunity you get."

"She's not my mother. She's just someone my father married."

"Exactly, and if you were nice to her your life would be much easier." He held up one hand as though to ward off my protest. "I know that's asking a lot of you right off, so you'll need to work your way up to it by throwing out little compliments. Tell her you like her outfits. That's something girls say to each other, and she spends enough time primping that it's got to be important to her."

"Are you through?"

"Lastly, you've got to ask her opinion on things. She considers herself an expert on everything, so it's like acknowledging she's the all-wise, all-seeing Yoda of the family."

"You're pathetic, Dante."

"Pathetic? I asked her opinion on the party refreshments, and now she's buying me one of those twelve-foot submarine sandwiches. A few more well-placed questions and she'll hire a band and a guy to do an ice sculpture in my likeness."

I picked up my fork and started in on my lasagna again.

"Yeah, well, don't get too attached to those ice sculptures, because somewhere down in hell the devil has a lounge chair with your name on it."

He smiled and shook his head. "I'm telling you, you make things harder than they have to be."

Yeah, probably, but what else was new?

Chapter

9

Even though we turned in our petitions to get Dante's name on the ballot, the office didn't let us start campaigning until the Monday of next week. Wilson didn't let up on his flirting at all, though. I even caught him once with Raine. They walked to lunch together, and she actually giggled at something he said. Raine is not the type of girl who giggles. She is not flighty, or flirty, and she never giggles.

Raine and Wilson went their separate ways in the cafeteria, and she walked the rest of the way to our table alone. She plopped down in her chair, blushing, and wouldn't look at me.

I tapped my fingers against the table. "Raine," I said.

Her head bobbed up in exasperation. "What? I only walked with him because I knew if he was with me, then he wouldn't be using his campaigning techniques on anyone else."

"You giggled," I said.

She took her sandwich out of her lunch sack. "Well, he's six three and gorgeous. Excuse me for having hormones."

Another one under his spell—and this time one of my friends. "Raine," I complained, "how could you?"

"I'm not going to marry him or anything." She took a bite of her sandwich, and her smile grew dreamy. "Although if he asked me to prom . . ."

"You'd still vote for Dante," Charity finished for her.

"Right," Raine said and hurriedly took another bite of her sandwich.

Daphne leaned toward Raine, excitement in her voice. "Did he actually mention the P word to you?"

Raine turned toward Daphne and lowered her voice. "He asked if I'd been asked yet. He seemed really interested, and when I told him I hadn't, he gave me this big smile—"

"That he uses on anyone who can vote," I added.

Daphne sent a glare in my direction.

"Well, it's true," I said.

Raine let out a sigh, fiddling with the straw to her milk. "I'm just glad he spoke to me. Have you all noticed that the popular kids are giving us the cold shoulder?"

Charity nodded. "Some of the girls at church told me I was committing social suicide." She glanced over at me. I must have looked startled, because her gaze turned consoling. "It didn't change my mind. I'll still campaign for Dante."

Raine nodded. "Dante has to win. That's all there is to it. The popular kids won't be able to snub us if he wins."

"They can still snub us," Charity said, "but they'll know that the masses support us instead of them—well, that is if the masses support us instead of them."

No one said anything for a moment. My stomach clenched, and I wondered if I'd be able to finish my lunch.

Daphne leaned back in her chair with a puzzled expression. "No one has criticized me about campaigning for Dante. In fact, Luke Talbot asked me to prom."

Which figured. Once again, Daphne's world was not our own. In her world it was perfectly logical that Wilson's best friend would want to be with her even though she was campaigning for his rival.

"What did you tell him?" I asked.

"I told him yes."

"But . . ." I didn't finish. How could I point out that this was offering aid and comfort to the enemy? She'd already said yes, and was halfway through a description of the prom dress she wanted.

She must have noticed I didn't say anything else, because after the prom dress description, she reached over and patted my arm. "Don't worry, Gi, we'll find a prom date for you. I think you'll really like Nathan."

In English class Mrs. Pembroke started the class by holding up every rejection letter she'd ever been sent. I couldn't believe anyone would keep them, let alone bring them to school and show them off, but she did.

She read a couple to us, then stapled all the letters to the bulletin board. She smacked the stapler against the paper with a lot of force, used way more staples than were needed, and muttered things under her breath we couldn't fully understand, like, "So how's my pacing now!" I was afraid this might be the beginning of a nervous breakdown, and next she'd start eating pencils, but she seemed fine after that, and class went on.

Over the rest of the week I looked at the bulletin board a lot. I know it's strange, but I felt an odd kinship with those letters. As though they had been written to me about my life, and I could make them all go away if Dante won the election.

Well, I told you it was strange.

I was all set to go to my grandma's house on Friday so Nathan could pick me up from there, but as it turned out,

Dad and Gabby had plans with some of her friends that night. They weren't even coming home after work and told us they'd probably be out late. Since no one would be home to catch me acting ungrounded—except for Dante and Skipper, both of whom I could bribe into secrecy using Snickers bars—there was no point in going to Grandma's house.

After the last two dates, I'd realized Grandma was a dangerous woman. I should have known this already, because when she met Jesse, she saw his motorcycle and asked if he belonged to a gang. Of course he said no, but you could tell she didn't believe him. She kept recounting episodes of *Law and Order* where gang members killed each other in shoot-outs.

Probably I shouldn't introduce her to any more of my love interests until sometime after my first wedding anniversary.

As I put on my makeup, Dante leaned against the bathroom door and examined the ceiling thoughtfully. "PlayStation or Xbox?" he asked me.

I rubbed a patch of smoky topaz eye shadow across one eyelid and then the other. "What are you talking about?"

"I'm wondering what I should ask for when Gabby finds out you went on a date."

"You'd better not tell her," I said.

"You'd better get back in before she comes home."

I ran my hands through my hair, fluffing it. "We're just going out to dinner. We'll be back in plenty of time. But if not, cover for me. Tell her I went to Charity's house to make posters for you."

"You can't drag Charity into this."

I blinked, then opened my eyes wide to put on a coat of mascara. I didn't say anything else.

"Sheesh, Giovanna, she's a minister's daughter. It has to be a double sin to make a minister's daughter lie for you."

This from the guy who teased her mercilessly that his motorcycle's name was the Demonmobile and was going to get her. I smiled, then turned each cheek to apply blush. "Don't worry. I won't get caught."

He shook his head. Sometimes Dante uses his six-minute head start into the world to pretend he's older and wiser than I am. "Just once. All you'd have to say is, 'Hey Gabby, that outfit looks stunning on you,' just once, and she'd probably lift your grounding."

"Well, maybe someday she'll wear a stunning outfit and I'll be in luck."

Dante did more head shaking and went downstairs.

Nathan picked me up at six o'clock. He had the build of a football player, but he didn't say he was one, and after my last blind date, I was afraid to ask. We made small talk for a few minutes in the living room, discussing where we should go to dinner, and then he said, "If you're up for an adventure, I know a great place."

I imagined some exotic cuisine. Thai food maybe, or sushi. "Sounds great," I said.

We walked outside to his truck. As we drove through town, my spirits rose. Daphne had finally found me a cool, outgoing, fun, passionate, understanding guy. The only thing more I could wish for was that Jesse would see me with him.

Then we pulled up to Warren's Bar & Grill. I had never been there, because it's a bar first and a grill second.

"They serve great ribs here," Nathan said as he turned off the ignition. "Have you ever ridden a mechanical bull?"

I didn't move from the truck. "Um, don't you have to be twenty-one to get in?"

He released his seatbelt and opened his door. "Yeah, but the bouncer is a friend of mine. You won't have a problem as long as you're with me." He stepped out of the truck, and I reluctantly followed, walking with small steps toward the door.

Nathan went on, filling the quiet with talk about the bar's band and how they had country swing lessons every Friday night. All I could think about was: *What will happen if I get caught during a police raid of this place?*

I mean, how serious was underage trespassing? For example, would Judge Rossmar—who'd gone into considerable detail about how I could be incarcerated if I got in trouble again—would he consider it a bad thing if I went into a bar?

I stopped a good ten feet in front of the door. Just stopped and stared at the building.

"What's wrong?" Nathan surveyed me, then put one hand on his hip. "Don't tell me—you hate country music, don't you?"

"No, it's just that it's illegal for a minor . . . and I'm already on probation and all—"

His eyebrows lifted. "You're on probation?"

This is not the kind of information you want to divulge on a first date, and he actually took a step away from me. "Probation for what?"

"Oh, not anything bad," I said quickly. "The school caught me with stolen frogs, but it wasn't my fault, and they were already dead . . ."

Which is also not something you want to tell a guy on the first date and probably didn't make the situation any better. "It's a long story," I said, "but I can't get in trouble again."

His gaze traveled from me to the front door and back again. "Okay, no trouble then." He let out a nervous laugh. "I promise not to start any barroom brawls if you don't."

My feet moved forward again. I needed to stop worrying about every little thing. Of course nothing bad would happen. The police didn't raid bars for no reason. Besides, I wouldn't actually drink or anything.

We walked inside and sure enough, no one carded us. The guy at the door and Nathan exchanged greetings and beyond that no one paid any attention to us.

I guess I'd expected the place to be some dark, cramped, smoke-filled room, with a bunch of broken-down, half-conscious men parked at the bar. Instead the room was big and well lit. To the side of the bar was a dance floor, eating area, and a pool table. Several planters with huge silk trees were scattered throughout the room, and pictures of horses lined the walls.

We walked slowly across the floor. "You want to play a little pool before we eat?" Nathan asked.

"I don't know how," I said.

He turned toward the back of the room where the pool table stood and motioned me to follow. "No problem. I can teach you."

I followed after him, feeling grown up. Here I was with a guy in a bar playing pool. So there, Jesse.

Nathan picked up two cue sticks and handed one to me. I leaned up against the table while he captured all of the balls inside a triangle thing.

"This is the eight ball," he told me, pointing to the black one. "It's the most important ball on the table. You've got to watch it carefully."

I don't know what made me look up right then. I mean, Nathan had just told me to watch the eight ball, but instead I glanced up.

It was then that I saw Dad, Gabby, and another couple coming straight across the room. They hadn't seen me, but stopped with their backs to the pool table and surveyed the place as though looking for somewhere good to sit.

I dropped to the ground, cue stick and all.

There is probably a reason children should pay attention to their parents' schedules, and if I ever sneaked out again I would definitely find out where Dad and Gabby planned on going first. But really, you couldn't blame me for being surprised. I mean, since when did they like country music, ribs, or pool? Granted, maybe I didn't know that much about what Gabby liked because I tried to block out her presence as much as possible, but still, the woman was in her forties. You wouldn't think she'd step foot in a place with a mechanical bull.

"Okay . . ." Nathan tilted his head to look at me. His voice took on that tone you use when you talk to small children. "What are you doing on the floor?"

I peered around the table's leg to see if my parents were still there. They were. If I had wanted to spit on Gabby's pink flowered heels, I could have. "Shhh," I told Nathan. "Pretend I'm not here."

He leaned down toward me, his eyes wide. "And where

am I supposed to pretend you are? The moon? The funny farm maybe?"

"Shhh," I said again. "Don't look at me."

He straightened, looked at the cue stick, then shot me another glance. "So, do you have some medication or something that I should know about?"

I motioned toward the pairs of legs on the other side of the table and mouthed the words, "Those are my parents."

"Oh." He nodded and lowered his voice. "And they won't be happy to see you in a bar? I can explain that we just came in for the ribs. It's not like we were drinking or anything."

I shook my head. "I'm supposed to be grounded right now."

He nodded again, more slowly. "Grounded, huh?"

Let me say right now that despite Daphne's assurances that she was setting me up with an understanding guy, she really hadn't.

An understanding guy would realize why I had to crawl over to the nearest planter, wait there until the coast was clear, and then dart out the front door like the place had caught on fire. An understanding guy would not pretend that he didn't know me as we walked across the parking lot, or act all ticked off because now his bouncer friend would think he was hitting on mentally challenged girls. I mean, I'm sure the people who noticed me crawling across the restaurant floor figured I had a legitimate reason for doing it. Like maybe I'd lost a rolling contact and was trying to find it. Up close and really fast.

I tried to laugh the whole thing off, but the ride back home was silent and awkward. The only thing Nathan said was, "So your parents don't let you out much. Any particular reason why?"

Like I was going to explain anything to him after all that.

*A*ll Saturday we cleaned for Dante's party. Gabby didn't buy any ice sculptures or hire a band, but she did decide on a theme for his party: Patriotic. Everything was done in red, white, and blue. The dishes, the tablecloth, the sugar cookies—her outfit. It was blue velour. We had star-spangled centerpieces and Fourth of July lights leading up to the doorstep from the sidewalk.

At seven thirty Raine, Charity, Stephen, and Brandon showed up. Gabby and Dad went upstairs. "But," Gabby told us pointedly, "we'll be down to check on you."

During the next half an hour a dozen freshman boys showed up, all of whom had signed my petition and seemed to think I personally wanted them to come hang out with me. And okay, I might have smiled when I asked them to sign their names, and maybe I'd flirted a little on account of being desperate to get my quota of signatures, but really, you'd think Dante would be grateful. But no, every time he passed me on my way somewhere trying to avoid or lose one of them, he'd say, "So tell me again how you don't use people like Wilson and I do?"

Yeah, I hoped Wilson was having as hard a time with all the girls he'd flirted with as I was having with my freshman groupies.

I tried to deflect some of the guys toward Charity and Raine, but Charity immediately pulled out her I-can't-date-until-I'm-sixteen defense to ward them off, and Raine invented a jealous boyfriend from Swain Academy. His name was Thor, and he spent all of his free time weight lifting and ripping off the limbs of guys who spoke to her.

If you ask me, Raine totally took the coward's way out, but if I'd thought of it first, I would have invented a story just like it. In fact, I would be dating Thor's twin brother, Zeus, and then we could double to prom.

But no, it didn't occur to me until it was too late to jump on the Thor bandwagon, so I was stuck with a constant herd of freshman guys encircling me.

Emily, the freshman girl who'd given her phone number to Dante, showed up with her friend, Isabella, and the two of them sat perched on the couch next to him, trying to out-flirt each other. They called him "Mr. President" and asked if he had any interns yet. This made Charity glare at him and mutter things into her drink.

Dante didn't notice her reaction. No one did, and I wondered how long this sort of thing had gone on before I'd picked up on it.

Daphne came with a guy named Derek from Swain, who was muscley enough that he might very well have spent a lot of time in the gym with Thor, but luckily none of the freshman guys asked.

At eight forty-five Dante cornered me in the kitchen. "Do you think these are all the people that will show? I've got your friends, my friends, and a small flock of freshmen. That's it."

I didn't know what to say, so I shrugged. "It's a cozy party. That's not a bad thing."

"I've got a twelve-foot sub sandwich in the kitchen that we've eaten a little over three feet of. We won't be able to fit the rest of it in the refrigerator. I'll have to go out looking for homeless people to give it to."

"No you won't. Those freshmen are skinny, but they eat a lot."

Dante clenched his jaw and looked at the table. The overflowing bowls of potato chips, the neatly arranged plates of cookies, the stacks of unused red, white, and blue dishes all seemed a pathetic reminder of our goal.

Wilson was going to win the election by a landslide. This meant my friends and I would see our social standing slide even further. My brother would carry around this experience as one more reason to be cynical about life, and I'd have to eat a pair of shoes.

Plus, after a week or so of leftovers, both Dante and I would have an aversion to submarine sandwiches and Fourth of July decorations for the rest of our lives.

Dante picked up the cordless phone and the white pages. "I'm calling anyone who answers their phone and personally inviting them here."

Well, as long as his plans didn't involve blazing potted palms, I wasn't going to protest.

A little after nine o'clock the doorbell rang and Dante let Rich, Brett, and Shane inside. They were part of the delinquent crowd at the high school. The type of kids who spent more time smoking in the parking lot than they ever spent in front of books. Mostly they wasted their weekends drinking, and apparently this weekend wasn't much different, since none of them appeared to be sober. "Hey, thanks for inviting us," Rich told Dante. "Wilson wouldn't let us in to his party with our friend."

"Your friend?" Dante asked.

"Yeah, our buddy Jack Daniel's." Then all three of them laughed like this was hilarious.

Brett leaned over and patted Dante on the shoulder like they'd known each other forever. "You've got our vote, man. You're the greatest."

Dante smiled stiffly and motioned them toward the

kitchen. "Well, you don't need your friend here. I've got nine feet of sandwich for you to eat."

The three stumbled off in that direction, talking to each other instead of us, until Shane called out, "Hey, you got any tequila?"

"No, but there's Cokes in the ice cooler," Dante said.

I sent him a "Gabby will freak out" look, but he ignored me and followed them into the kitchen. Maybe to keep them from going through our cupboards. None of them came out again, so I assumed they either were in there eating or had passed out.

Emily and Isabella kept throwing looks in the direction of the kitchen, as though they wanted to go in after Dante. I decided to do Charity a favor. While I changed out CDs in the stereo, I called Brandon and Stephen over to me. "See those two girls sitting on the couch? They're really impressed with upperclassmen. You should go talk to them."

Brandon glanced at the girls, then back at me. "I thought Dante liked one of them."

I shook my head. "No, he likes someone else. In fact, it's a little awkward for him to have those two tagging around after him all night."

Stephen smiled lazily. "I think we could help him out then."

Brandon let his gaze rest on them, appraising them with

a satisfied nod. "Maybe they'd like to catch a late movie. You know, as a favor to Dante."

The two went over and sat by the girls, and I started a new CD playing. By the time the first song ended, the four of them headed out the door. I hoped Dante wouldn't notice, and if he did notice, that he wouldn't be too mad at me.

I walked toward the family room so I could talk to Charity, but before I made it there, three freshman guys cornered me. I may have been stuck there indefinitely, listening to their opinions on Final Fantasy, but after a few minutes Daphne emerged from the family room and came over to rescue me. She smiled at the guys, said, "Excuse me, I need Giovanna for a minute—you know, for girl stuff," and plucked me from their midst.

We walked upstairs to my room. I would have been relieved, except I knew she wanted to talk to me about my date with Nathan, which—let's face it—was not going to be pretty. I mean, if Nathan hadn't told her how it went, then I was going to have to do it. And there is no good way to explain to your friend that the date she arranged for you ended with the guy comparing you to the mentally challenged.

I sat down on one end of my bed, and she sat down on the other. She forced a smile at me. "Well, they say, 'The course of true love never did run smooth.' "

"That's right," I said.

"However, you may have noticed that they never say anything about hiding under a pool table and crawling across the restaurant on your hands and knees."

"It didn't happen like that—"

She held up both hands to stop me. "It doesn't matter. It's all history now. We just have to move on and find someone who doesn't know Nathan, so they can't compare notes. That might be a little difficult, since from what I understand, rumors of your date are already making the rounds of Swain Academy."

I put my hand to my forehead. My head suddenly hurt. "He told people about our date?"

"Giovanna, you let the guy know you'd been arrested for stealing dead frogs and then crawled underneath a pool table. You didn't think he'd tell people about it?"

I gulped and felt my face flush. "If he was a gentleman, he wouldn't have told—Jesse wouldn't have."

"Well, you broke up with Jesse."

Her statement hit me hard. I'd broken up with Jesse, and yet I suddenly realized that despite everything, I wanted him back. Forget loyalty. Forget this stupid election. I just wanted my boyfriend back.

Daphne reached over and momentarily put her hand over mine to get my attention. "It will all be fine. You just need some prep work for your next date. You know, a game plan of what to say and how to act." She let out a sigh, but not one of resignation. This was the breath you let out before you tackled something huge. "I've gone about this matchmaker business all wrong. I've tried to set you up with guys I thought would be good for you. But I never found out what you're looking for. So let's start with that. We want to find someone who is absolutely compatible. So you tell me, what do you want in a guy?"

"Jesse," I said.

"You want a guy like Jesse?"

"No, I want him. I want Jesse back."

Daphne's lips twitched in frustration. "But I thought you were mad because he'd betrayed Dante's trust."

"I am. I want him to be sorry when he comes back, but mostly I just want him back."

"You want your ex-boyfriend . . ." Daphne tapped her fingers across my quilt.

I bit my lip, watching her expression change from frustration to doubt. Almost to herself she murmured, "That won't be easy."

"But you told me you didn't think he was over me, because he doesn't want me to date other guys. So isn't there a way we could take the ex out of ex-boyfriend?"

"Hmmm." Daphne stood up and turned around my

room. She crossed her arms and looked, unseeing, at my window. I didn't say anything, because I didn't want to disturb her thought process.

Finally she turned back to me. "He'll have to think it's his idea. That's the thing about guys. They love a challenge. If you come crawling back to him, it's like admitting you aren't capable of doing better. He'll think you're a B-list girl. Then the only way to salvage his dignity—so he's not lumped together with all the guys who wouldn't have you—is to dump you right back. I mean, he's already got Bridget itching for an invitation to prom, and most guys think she's A-list."

Without meaning to, I clutched the side of my quilt. The situation suddenly seemed very bleak. I mean, with probation, and now the pool table incident—exactly how far down in the alphabet had I fallen? I was probably languishing somewhere down by Q.

"Daphne, I'm not A-list material."

Daphne let out a snort and waved one hand to dismiss my objection. "No one is, Giovanna. It's all perception. The trick is to make other people think you're A-list."

"How do I do that?"

She sat down on the bed again, looking at me intently to emphasize her point. "Well, first off, you've got to think it yourself."

"I'm supposed to act snobby?"

"No, not snobby. Snobby people might as well walk around with a sign that says, 'Look at me—I'm trying to be A-list.' You have to like yourself, that's all. When you like yourself, you have confidence. Confidence is an A-list quality."

"Confidence." I sat up straighter to show her I was trying.

"And of course you'll need to go clothes shopping."

"Shopping? What's wrong with my clothes?"

She tilted her head at me. "Nothing is wrong with them. They just could be more . . . right. We'll talk about your hair later."

My hand automatically went to my head. "What's wrong with my hair?"

"Later," she said.

It was suddenly hard to have confidence.

"And of course we'll have to set you up with some guys from Swain."

Even the word *Swain* made me cringe. "But I just told you I want Jesse back—"

"Exactly," she said. "And it's a well-known fact that nothing makes a girl more attractive to an ex-boyfriend than to see her with a new guy. It's that whole challenge thing. We'll find out where Jesse is going to be this week and make sure you're there too with a totally A-list guy."

"Okay," I said. I had no idea how to find out where

Jesse would be, and only knew it wouldn't be at my house since Gabby had banished him, and I was still grounded. Right now Jesse was at Wilson's house, which I couldn't go to, even though my mind had made frequent stops there all evening.

I pictured Jesse sitting in the hot tub with Bridget. Bridget no doubt wore an A-list bikini on her double-D body, while both of them ate caviar on crackers shaped in the words "Vote for Wilson."

A knock sounded on my door, then Charity's voice filtered in. "Giovanna, are you in there?"

"Yeah, come in. Daphne and I were just talking about . . ." I glanced over at Daphne, reluctant to say more. "Some stuff."

Charity cracked open the door. "Daphne, Derek is acting bored, and I think he wants to leave. Giovanna, you need to get downstairs, because Rich and his friends are acting like idiots, and Dante isn't doing anything to stop them."

Okay, great. What was I supposed to do about the three drunk guys my brother invited to the party? It should be his problem, not mine. Still, I trudged out of my room and down the stairs. If Gabby found drunk guys at our party, she'd probably veto any other parties for the duration of our teenage years.

Several more people had come. Mostly they were fringe kids, the ones who didn't fit in with any of the cliques at school. There were also more freshmen and a few foreign exchange students who probably didn't have enough of a grasp of the English language to understand anything either Dante or Wilson said about the election.

Rich, Brett, and Shane stood in the middle of the group re-enacting a scene from *The Matrix*. Or at least they tried. Mostly Rich fell down instead of dodging the imaginary bullets that Brett and Shane shot at him.

The foreign kids kept looking at those three, then talking among themselves. They probably wondered about the American party game that required guests to swoop around and then fall on the floor. They looked a little worried as they spoke to each other, like maybe next we'd ask them to perform in this strange ritual. I bet they all wrote some interesting letters back home this week.

I took hold of Dante's arm. "Can I talk to you?"

"Sure," he said. He didn't get to say much more before I dragged him into the kitchen.

Once there I let my gaze bore into him. "You've got to get rid of Rich, Brett, and Shane before Gabby comes downstairs to check on the party."

Dante shrugged off my hand. "They're harmless."

"She'll think they got drunk here. Remember how she

gave us that big lecture about how serving alcohol to minors is illegal and how I can't afford to get in trouble with the law again?"

Dante rolled his eyes. Easy for him not to worry. He hadn't already imagined up a life in prison with a tiny cell, a rickety bunk bed, and a two-hundred-pound roommate who thrashed in her sleep.

"I can't just send them home," he said. "They're wasted. They'll hit every telephone pole from here to the other side of Bickham."

I waited for him to say more. He didn't. "So what were you planning? Letting them sleep it off on the living room floor? Gabby will love that."

He held up both hands—the exact same gesture Grandma used before breaking into Italian. "Well, we can't take them home now. We can't leave our own party."

"We?" I asked. "We?"

"Sure. After the party you can drive them home in their car. I'll follow you on my bike, so when you drop off their car I can take you back home."

I stared at him. "You want me to get in a car with three drunk guys? Hello, I wouldn't trust those guys when they were sober."

His tone turned impatient. "Fine. I'll ask Brandon or Stephen to do it."

Well, that probably meant Dante would notice I'd sent

them away. I hesitated, looking at the refreshments instead of my brother. "Oh, um, they already left."

Dante tilted his head. "They left? Why?"

I couldn't lie about it. I knew he'd ask his friends about it later. "I sort of told them they should talk to Emily and Isabella, and I think they all went to see a movie."

"They went to a—" He took two steps toward the living room, as though about to go after them, then turned back to me. "Why did you tell them to do that?"

"Because you're the host of the party, and I didn't think you wanted those girls hanging off you like little freshman barnacles."

Dante's hands went back up in the air. "Why would you think that?"

"I thought you liked someone else."

"I've never told you that I . . ." He took a step back toward me, and I could almost see him processing through the implications. "What you mean is you want me to like someone else."

I let out a snort as though the idea was ridiculous, but he nodded and took another step closer to me. His eyes narrowed. "And it must be someone at this party, or you wouldn't have sent those girls packing."

It figured. Just when I didn't want Dante to know what I was up to, the whole twin-psychic-bond thing kicked in. It was like Dante was peering into my head and seeing everything. I tried to block out Charity's name from my mind. I thought of unicorns and ice cream cones and beach balls.

He nodded, and his expression grew tighter. "It can't be Daphne, because she's here with a guy."

Starfish, and clam shells, and those seaweedy things that wash up on the beach.

Another thought occurred to me. Maybe Dante had been able to read my mind all along, and he'd just never found anything in it interesting enough to comment on before. That would be so like him.

He took another step toward me and folded his arms. "It can't be Charity, because she doesn't date yet. You're trying to set me up with Raine, aren't you?"

"No," I said.

He tossed his head back and groaned. "Yes, you are. Have you talked to her about me? Does she like me?"

"No," I said.

More groaning. "Oh, crap. Now it's going to be all weird being around her. Is she expecting me to ask her to prom?"

"I'm not trying to set you up, Dante. Don't be so full of yourself."

He put his hand over his forehead and shut his eyes. "How could you do this to me? I'm going to have to avoid her until she finds someone else to like."

"Well, that shouldn't be too hard for her, Prince Charming."

Dante turned back around to leave. I took a step to follow him. We both noticed Charity standing in the doorway at the same time. I wasn't sure how much of our conversation she'd heard, but judging from the fact that the color had completely left her face, I figured she'd heard enough.

"I came to tell you that Rich is getting out of control," she said.

Dante's expression grew even darker. "Oh. Thanks. We'll take care of it." He strode past her out into the family room. I walked past her too. She gave me a vicious glare as I did, but there wasn't time to explain anything to her.

As we walked into the living room, I noticed several things wrong. The first was that Rich stood on our coffee table waving, and very nearly spilling, a glass full of Coke.

He tossed his head back and belted out a song that had something to do with eating worms from tequila bottles and bathing in Jack Daniel's. Brett and Shane sat on the floor in front of him like judges from *American Idol* and yelled up comments about his performance. Mostly they used the phrase, "You suck, man!"

The second thing wrong, and this was nearly as important, was that Skipper stood not two feet away from them, dancing and laughing at Rich's song. She sang the words to her own song, which went, "Worms, worms, worms, Jack Daniel's." This was especially bad, even though she had better rhythm and was more in key than Rich.

But worst of all, I heard my parents' bedroom door shut, and then footsteps coming across the upstairs hallway. I wasn't sure what Gabby's reaction to the scene in front of me would be, but I knew it probably would involve a lot of yelling.

Chapter

11

Dante took hold of my arm to get my attention. "I'll get Rich off the table. You take Skipper back upstairs."

I didn't answer him. I just hurried over to Skipper and picked her up. "C'mon Skip, it's past your bedtime."

Her lips scrunched into a pout. "But I wanna dance on the table too."

I hurried to the stairs. "Mommy wouldn't like that, so we're not going to tell her we saw anyone doing it at Dante's party, okay?"

I made it up three stairs before Gabby came down. She saw us, quickened her step, and held out her arms to Skipper. "What are you doing out of bed?"

The pout dropped from Skipper's lips. She reached out her hands to Gabby and batted her lids tiredly. "I tried to sleep, but they were too loud."

Gabby's gaze switched to me. "Yes, I came downstairs to tell them the same thing."

"Sorry," I said. "Dante's taking care of it."

I waited for her to turn around and take Skipper back upstairs. She didn't. Instead her gaze traveled past me to the crowd in the family room.

Luckily, no one was dancing on the coffee table, or had spilled large quantities of soda on the carpet. Rich stood with his friends in the middle of the room raising his plastic cup with a wobbly hand. In a voice much too loud to let a five-year-old sleep, he said, "I want to offer a toast to our next pres-i-Dante."

Brett waved him off. "No more singing, man. You suck."

Rich tried to push him away, but missed. "I'll break your teeth out, and then we'll see who sucks."

Gabby let out disapproving huff and took a step downstairs. I didn't move out of the way. "By the way, Gabby, I've been meaning to tell you I love your outfit."

She pushed past me as though she hadn't heard me, and I followed her to the foot of the stairs.

Rich raised his glass. "To Dante, you're going to-quila Wilson on election day." He let out a laugh and added, "'Cause Wilson don't know Jack . . . Daniel's."

There was miscellaneous clapping and hoots of agreement, mostly from Brett and Shane.

"Is that boy drunk?" Gabby asked.

"Oh, him? No, that's just Rich. Since his pole vaulting accident last year, he doesn't make much sense anymore, but we all humor him anyway."

Shane raised his glass. "No worms are good worms!"

More clapping. Gabby's lips twisted into a disapproving frown.

"That's Shane," I told her. "He's the one who fell off the pole vault onto Rich."

Gabby put her hand on Skipper's head and turned to me. "I'm going to put your sister to bed. When I come back down, I want those boys gone from my house. Do you understand?"

I nodded.

"Good." She turned around and walked up the stairs. Over her shoulder Skipper gave me a wave good-bye and sang, "Worms, worms, worms."

I trudged downstairs, trying to figure out how to get Rich, Shane, and Brett home. Dante couldn't leave his own party, but if Daphne's date drove them in Shane's car, then I could follow behind him in mine.

I took a deep breath. It would work. Derek had enough muscle that he could handle three drunks. I walked around the room searching for Derek and Daphne but didn't see either one of them. Charity and Raine, however, stood together at one end of the room. Raine picked her purse up from the couch and riffled through its contents. "Hey Giovanna, it's getting late, and Charity needs me to take her home—"

"Where's Derek and Daphne?" I asked.

Raine took her keys from her purse. "They left already."

"They left?" I repeated. "But I need them."

Raine raised an eyebrow. Charity faced the crowd and wouldn't look at me.

Dante strode up to us. "What did Gabby say?"

"She wants the drunks gone by the time she comes back downstairs."

Dante looked around the room, doing the same sort of calculations I'd just done. "Let's see, who can drive? Not your freshman admirers . . ."

"I'll drive Shane's car to his house." I didn't want to, but I didn't see another option. "Raine, can you please follow me in your car to give me a ride back home?"

"Okay," she said.

Dante nodded. "Great. I'll tell the guys the party is about to end and you're driving them home."

Charity finally spoke, but not to me, to Dante. "You can't put your sister in a car with three drunk guys. That has 'Bad Idea' written all over it."

"She's a good driver," Dante said.

"Yeah, be sure to mention that in her eulogy."

Dante let out one of the tormented sighs he saves for conversations with Charity. "She's not going to crash."

Charity's eyes flashed with frustration. "I'm not worried about her crashing. I'm worried about her body turning up in a shallow grave after those three Neanderthals flee the country."

"Um, you guys . . ." I said, not really because I had anything to say, but because it felt weird standing there—invisible—while they argued about me. Neither of them looked at or listened to me, though.

Dante took a rigid step toward Charity. "Do you want me to send along some of her freshman friends to protect her?"

"No, I want you to drive the guys home. You invited them. They're your responsibility."

"Fine," he said. "I'll leave my own party, and Giovanna and the rest of you can stay here to entertain my guests."

Raine jingled her keys. "Except for me. I've got to go with you so you have a ride back home."

Dante looked at her. He didn't say anything for a moment, but I could tell he was thinking about the ride home with her. The two of them alone the whole way. The conversation he would have to try and come up with.

Dante narrowed his eyes at Charity. "You want me to go with Raine, is that it?"

She shrugged. "Yep, pretty much."

"Well, isn't that convenient," he said. Meaning, I suppose, that he thought Charity was in on the conspiracy to set him up with Raine.

"I can drive the guys home," I said. "It's really no problem."

Dante kept his eyes on Charity. His words came out with forced politeness. "There you have it; Giovanna wants to do it herself. What's a concerned brother to do?"

I took Raine's arm. "Come on. The sooner we leave, the sooner it will be over."

Raine walked beside me toward the door, but looked back over her shoulder. "What was that all about? Dante's acting weird all of a sudden."

"Guys do that sometimes."

As we walked outside, Charity caught up to us. "I'll come with you, Giovanna. I'll have two free hands to use my cell phone, so at least I'll be able to call for help if they attack us."

"Great," I said. "The more the merrier." I'd seen Shane's PT Cruiser in the school parking lot. I walked up and peered inside the car. A couple of crumpled cans lay in the back along with a suspiciously empty bottle. How much of this stuff could they drink and still stay conscious?

Raine walked over to her Taurus and slipped in behind the wheel.

A minute later Dante came out with the guys. Shane and Brett both swayed as they walked. Dante had a hold of

Rich's arm to keep him steady. "The night is still young," Rich slurred out. "We have hours left to party."

Dante steered Rich to the back seat of Shane's car. "And you can party at your house, because my parents want to send you home now. But thanks for coming."

"Parents suck," Brett said. Dante helped him into the car and then turned to Shane for the keys.

Shane fished around in his jacket pocket and then his other pocket, and then his jeans pocket. Finally, he produced them. He gave them to me and stumbled into the back seat with his friends.

Charity got into the front seat without telling Dante good-bye. He watched her for a moment, his face unreadable, and then stalked back to the house.

I pulled onto the street, and Raine followed me. "Okay guys, whose house am I taking you to?"

This caused an eruption of laughter from the back seat. "Mine," Rich said.

"No, it's my house," Brett said. And they all laughed again.

Drunk people are so strange.

"Where do you live, Shane?" I asked, because it would be easiest to take the car there and let Shane's parents worry about the guys.

"I'll give you directions," he said. "Go down this street."

"Remember to stop at the stop sign," Brett said.

"And then go again," Rich added.

A shuffling noise came from the back seat. "Is there anything to drink back here?" Brett asked.

"Man, if you stopped stepping on my hands I could tell you," Rich said.

I tried to block them out as much as I could except for the pertinent directions, like which roads to turn on. They always told me these between fits of laughter. Then they started up the worm song again.

Charity sat silently beside me, her cell phone open and the number 9-1-1 already pushed. Her finger hovered over the send button.

"So," I said to her, "besides all of this, did you think it was a fun party?"

She gave me a humorless stare. In a near whisper she hissed out, "I can't believe you told Dante I liked him."

"I didn't tell him."

Charity tried to blink away the emotion in her eyes. "You said something to him, because he said he'd feel all weird around me, and he'd have to avoid me until I liked someone else."

"That wasn't you. He was talking about Raine."

Her mouth dropped open, and she leaned toward me. "Raine likes him too?"

"No."

More laughter from the back seat. "Turn left at the light," Shane yelled. I turned from downtown Bickham, up the hill to a residential area. I hoped Charity would let the subject drop, but she didn't.

"If Raine doesn't like Dante, why did he say all those things about her?"

I hesitated, reluctant to admit my scheming, but there was no way around it. "Because I sent the freshman girls off with Stephen and Brandon, so he figured out that one of my friends liked him."

She didn't say anything for a moment. Her foot tapped against the floor. "You must have said something else, because just sending off two freshman girls isn't enough to trigger that lightbulb above his head to flicker on. I've been flirting with him since you moved in, and he hasn't figured out that I like him."

I resisted the urge to take my eyes off the road and stare at her. "Charity, when have you ever flirted with Dante?"

She let out a grunt of protest. "I talk to him all of the time. I help him with his calculus homework." She waved one hand at the darkness to emphasize her point. "I'm constantly telling him to be careful on his motorcycle and to stop hanging out with people who skip school."

"That's not really flirting. That's more like trying to reform him."

"Well, I'm doing it in a flirting way."

I turned on a street that led to Bickham's most exclusive neighborhood. I hadn't realized Shane lived in such an upscale place, and I hoped he didn't live on one of those estates that was surrounded by vicious guard dogs. "Look, Charity, I didn't say anything to him. But since we're twins, we may have a bond that allows him to read my mind. I'm not sure about that yet."

Charity folded her arms, her expression turning to resignation. "He'll probably ask Raine to prom now that he thinks she likes him. After all, she's pretty and tall."

Shane leaned over the back of the seat. I could smell him before he spoke. "It's that house right over there."

Mansion was more like it. I pulled farther down the road but didn't see a place to park. Vehicles lined the streets, and the driveway already had cars in it.

"Why are there so many cars here?" Charity asked.

Which only made the guys laugh all over again. Did I already mention how strange drunk people are? If so, it's worth repeating.

Brett rolled down his window and yelled out, "We're home!"

And then I saw them. The people standing on the porch. The potted palms lining the walk. I gripped the steering wheel. "This is Wilson's house."

Rich leaned over the seat. "Hey, a party is a party. You wanna be our dates? I bet they'd let you all in."

Charity turned around and glared at him. "You think this is funny? We ought to leave you here."

The idea was tempting. We could kick them out of the car and let them walk home. Only then they might call the police and report that I'd stolen their car. That would be bad.

See, you know your life is messed up when you don't think in terms of whether something is right or wrong, but by how many years in jail it would get you.

"Look in the glove box for a registration slip," I told Charity. "That should have Shane's address on it."

Charity opened the glove box, and I slowly eased past Wilson's house, hoping none of the people out on his porch could recognize me.

Brett stuck his head out of the open window, flung an empty bottle toward the house, and yelled, "How do you like Jack now?"

I heard the crash. I wasn't sure if it was a window or just the bottle breaking against Wilson's driveway. The sound made my stomach twist inside of me.

"Why did you do that?" I yelled, and stepped on the gas. I wasn't sure where the street led to, but I couldn't back up, because Raine was right behind me. I hurried down the street, driving down the middle so I didn't sideswipe any of the parked cars. Brett still hung out the window, hollering some sort of war cry at the top of his lungs.

"Sit down and shut up!" I shouted.

He ignored me, and his war cry turned into some sort of werewolf-howling-at-the-moon thing. I checked over my shoulder, trying to see Wilson's house. "That was at least littering, and maybe vandalism! Those are probably misdemeanors, you know."

Charity riffled through the contents of the glove box. "There's all sorts of junk in here. What does a registration look like?"

"It's a little piece of paper."

Charity's phone rang. She pushed the speaker button, laid it on her lap, and kept riffling through the glove box. "Hello?"

Raine's voice came over the phone. "Are you all insane? I can't believe I just followed you to Wilson's house and watched you hurl a bottle at his guests. A little competition is one thing, but this is taking it too far."

I picked up the phone, took it off speaker, and held it to my face. "I didn't throw the bottle—that was Brett. Couldn't you tell the difference? His arms are way hairier than mine."

"Oh, sorry. My mistake. You can explain that to the people who ran outside after the bottle crashed on the driveway, because I think some of them got in their cars."

I looked in my rearview mirror, but I could only see Raine's Taurus. "Are you serious? Is anyone following us?"

"I don't see anyone yet," she said. "Oh wait, there's a truck behind me."

I turned on the first street I came to, and then the next, trying to find an outlet back to downtown. Nothing looked familiar. Suddenly I wasn't even sure that I knew what direction I was headed.

Raine's voice came over the phone. "Giovanna, do you have any idea where you're going?"

"Not really."

"I'm following you and you're lost?"

"I'm not lost. I just don't know where I'm supposed to go next." I handed the phone back to Charity. She set it down on her lap and turned on the overhead light. Then she picked up a handful of papers from the glove compartment and went through it like confetti. "Tire warranty . . . Oil-change receipt . . . I told Dante he should drive, but no . . ."

In the back seat all the guys gave each other high fives. If I hadn't been gripping the steering wheel, I would have turned around and slapped them. I finally found a street that led back to downtown. I let out a ragged breath of relief and sped up as I headed there.

"Here it is," Charity said. "He lives at twelve-seventeen Sycamore Street."

I flipped off the overhead light. "Sycamore . . . Sycamore. Do you know where that is?"

Charity shrugged. "No."

Rich leaned over the seat and said, "I'll tell ya how to get there. Take a U-turn at the next light." Or at least he tried to say it. He broke out laughing halfway through the sentence. Charity pushed him back into his own seat again.

I picked up the phone and asked Raine.

"It's somewhere in the tree streets," she said. "North of here."

I pulled onto Main Street, which is two lanes each direction. I knew whoever was following us would try to overtake us here. Luckily, since it was now ten thirty and downtown Bickham doesn't have much of a night life, the streets were mostly empty. I gunned the engine, zipping down the street, and made a sharp turn onto State Street.

Through the phone I heard Raine's voice edged with panic. "This isn't the way to the tree streets. Where are you going?"

"I'm trying to lose whoever is following us. That way Wilson will think Rich, Brett, and Shane went by his house and were being jerks again. He won't know we had anything to do with this, because we're in Shane's car, and it was Brett who yelled things out the window."

The panic rose in Raine's voice. "But I'm in my own car. Do you think Wilson recognized me? I mean, he hinted he might ask me to prom."

"Raine, Wilson hinted that he might ask everyone to prom. If he asks everyone he flirted with, he'll show up to the dance with a harem." At the last minute, and mostly because the green turn arrow flashed on, I turned and doubled back onto Main Street. Then I sped up to make it past a minivan.

"I'm hanging up now," Raine said. "I need to use two hands to drive if I'm going to keep up with you."

From the back seat the guys all chanted, "Drag race! Drag race!"

Charity checked the rearview mirror on her side of the car. "The truck is gaining on us."

Brett leaned his head out the window again. At first I thought he was going to throw up, but no, he just screamed again. "We can take you! Bring it on, buddy!"

Charity glanced at the speedometer. "It's dangerous to speed like this."

"I'm not going to crash." After pulling around the mini-van, I cut past an SUV, then sped through a light that was so yellow it was orange. I made a quick right turn onto Grand Street. I searched in the mirror but couldn't distinguish one pair of headlights from another. "Did we lose them?"

"You lost Raine, but the truck is still following us."

Not good. I switched lanes and took a sharp left. "She knows Shane's address. She'll probably go there."

Charity tilted her head, examining the rearview mirror again. "Um, Giovanna, what kind of truck does Jesse drive?"

"A white Ford."

"Yeah. I thought so."

There was a moment of silence—well, at least silence between Charity and me. I could feel my heart pounding in my chest.

"Please tell me that isn't Jesse following us," I said.

"I won't tell you if you don't want me to."

I looked into the rearview mirror and let out an involuntary scream. Yep. It was Jesse. Luke Talbot sat beside him.

The light in front of me turned red. The cross traffic started across the street. I couldn't do anything but stop at the intersection and wait. Jesse changed lanes and pulled up beside me. Yeah, this just kept getting better. I put my hand across the side of my face so I didn't have to look at him. I could hear him, though. He'd rolled down his window and yelled my name.

I slumped down in my seat and still didn't look over.

"Jesse knows now. You might as well talk to him," Charity said. She turned and waved at him.

"I want to die," I said.

Charity's cell phone rang. Without looking, I knew it was Jesse. He probably had called to congratulate me on the new breed of guys I was hanging out with now that I'd broken up with him. Charity answered it. "Hey, we can explain all of this—we're just taking these guys home because they're too drunk to drive."

A pause. Why did red lights last so long?

"Because they tricked us into going to Wilson's house," Charity said. "We had no idea they were going to throw that bottle."

Pause.

Charity cast a glance at me. "Well, we found Shane's address off his registration, so we're taking them home now."

Another pause. Surely the light should have changed by now. The cross traffic was long gone.

Charity turned around to check on the back seat, then put her hand over her eyes and spun back forward. "Okay, I'll let her know."

"What?" I asked.

"Jesse says to tell you that the guys are mooning all the cars you just passed, including a police car that's pulling up behind you."

I'd like to say here that Jesse has a terrific sense of humor, and it was all a joke that we laughed about, you know, once I'd recovered from my heart attack. But no. I spun around and sure enough, Rich, Brett, and Shane had various parts of their body pressed up against the windows. And although I imagine it wasn't a pretty sight for the people outside, trust me, it was worse looking at them from the inside of the car.

The light turned green, but it only barely registered in my mind. I let out a scream, picked up junk from the glove box, and pelted them with it. "PUT YOUR CLOTHES ON! ALL OF YOU!"

Instead of doing anything constructive, like, say, hiking their jeans back up, the three of them laughed so hard that, if anything, their pants slid closer to their ankles.

Someone honked, probably to remind me that the light had turned green, and I sat forward again and drove through the intersection. That was about as far as I got before the police car turned on its lights.

Chapter 12

The sobriety tests they give you in real life are not at all like the ones they show on TV. I was totally prepared to walk a straight line, and even a little nervous about it because I'm not really coordinated and was afraid I would trip or something and then the policeman would never believe I was sober—especially if I started spontaneously weeping, which I was very close to doing without walking the line.

But instead he marched us out of the car, took down our names, phone numbers, addresses, and then smelled our breath.

The guys flunked this test in a big way, and he sent them to sit in the back of his police car. After that, he took Charity a few feet away to discuss the matter with her.

She used a lot of hand-waving while talking to him. He wrote things down on a pad of paper and nodded grimly.

Then he talked to her. She mostly kept her gaze on the ground and looked like she was about to cry. This went on for quite some time.

I watched the two of them and felt ill. It was all my fault. She had just been an innocent passenger who came along to make sure I didn't end up in a shallow grave, and now she was being interrogated by a police officer. And if he was this stern with her, what was he going to say to me, the driver, who by the way was already on probation? My insides felt like they'd tangled themselves up and gotten lodged somewhere around the vicinity of my throat.

Finally the officer walked over to me. He slipped his pen back onto his clipboard and folded his arms. "First off, miss, I want to tell you that you did the right thing not to let those boys get behind the wheel tonight. You may have saved their lives and the life of whoever they would have hit when they tried to drive home. Because of that, I'm overlooking the speeding violation I would have otherwise given you."

With that one sentence most of my insides fell back into place. I would not be explaining all of this to Judge Rossmar. I wanted to cry with relief. I gulped out, "Thank you, officer."

"However, next time something like this happens, I want you to call a cab for your friends, okay?"

"Yes sir," I said.

"And I don't ever want to see you trying to outrun another vehicle, even if your ex-boyfriend is driving it, okay?"

"Okay." I glanced over at Charity, surprised she'd told him that part of the story.

After that the police called the guys' parents, and using words like, "underage alcohol consumption" and "disorderly conduct," told them they had to come down and pick up their sons.

Raine picked us up, and we headed to Charity's house to drop her off. No one spoke for a long time.

Finally I said, "It could have been worse."

Charity looked straight out the window with her arms folded. "The policeman who stopped you goes to my church. I'm going to have to face him every Sunday from now until I leave for college."

"Oh. Sorry."

"And of course I'll see him when I come home for Christmas."

"It's not like you really did anything wrong."

She leaned her head against the car door. "And for the summer break between college semesters."

"He probably sees a lot of this stuff and won't remember it past tomorrow."

Charity sent me an incredulous look. "He knows my father, Giovanna. They talk. I doubt either one of them will forget the night he pulled over the minister's daughter in a car full of drunk, half naked teenage boys."

Well, she did have a point. Still, it didn't seem fair that anyone should hold it against her. I held up one hand, offering her an argument she could use. "You were trying to do a good deed. Your father will understand." At least I hoped he would. I hoped he wouldn't label me as some juvenile delinquent troublemaker who shouldn't hang around his daughter anymore.

After Raine let Charity out, she drove me home. When I trudged into my house, Dante was cleaning up from the party. As I dragged myself into the kitchen, he eyed me over and said, "That sure took you long enough."

Which was the last straw. So I let him have it. I told him everything that had happened, including that it was his fault for inviting those drunk-mooning-idiots in the first place, and if Charity could never come over to our house again, that would be his fault too, and then I quit as his campaign manager. Again. Considering the school counselor thinks I have a hard time expressing anger, I did an exceptional job of telling Dante how I felt.

He held up both hands as though to ward off my words. "Okay, okay, I'm sorry." Then he shook his head. "But what's with you that you can't walk out of the house without getting in trouble with the law?"

I didn't answer him. I just walked up the stairs repeating, "I quit. I quit. I quit."

On Monday Dante and I went to school early to put up his posters. Technically I shouldn't have had to do this, since I had quit as his campaign manager. I reminded him of this fact about ten times the night before while we made more posters. Dante doesn't always take what I say seriously, though, and apparently ten times didn't convince him that I shouldn't have to trace his name onto posterboard.

So there I was up on a ladder taping up all of our nice, but obviously homemade, signs next to Wilson's mass-produced-by-someone-with-a-degree-in-graphic-design signs. They all showed these huge glossy pictures of Wilson smiling under the caption, "Leadership. Trust. Responsibility." At the bottom of the poster was a box with the words, "My promise to you," and a paragraph about how Wilson was all about service and so on and so on. This part was in his own handwriting, which I thought looked out of place. The whole thing had perfectly formatted lettering, and Wilson's up-and-down scrawl stuck out like a sore thumb.

And I'm not just saying this because I'm bitter that I had to trace the letters off of stencils to write, "Dante Is Our Man. Vote For El Pres-i-Dante," like, twenty times.

And yes, we did steal the term "pres-i-Dante" from our drunk party guests. It was catchier than anything we could come up with on our own.

So anyway, I was on the top of a ladder taping up posters when Bridget strolled by. She shot me one of her rodeo queen smiles. "I heard you had quite a party on Saturday."

I ripped off a piece of masking tape and marveled at the fact that Bridget had been able to find anyone who actually went to our party in order to talk to them about it. "Yeah," I said.

"I hear Rich, Brett, and Shane got smashed at your house."

My stomach lurched. "No, actually they arrived that way."

"That's not the way I heard it. Did you really go out partying with them afterward and get arrested?"

This is not something you should say to a person who's standing on the top of a ladder. I came dangerously close to toppling off. As I grasped onto the top rung, I sputtered out, "No, that didn't happen."

"The police didn't pull you over while you were speeding around downtown in Shane's car?"

"Well yeah, but we weren't partying, and we didn't get arrested. At least I didn't."

She shrugged her shoulders and blinked up at me. "See,

that's what I mean. Nothing that exciting happened at our party—well, except for when you all came by and threw a bottle at Wilson's house."

I held onto the ladder tighter, too shocked by the speed of the rumors to care that she was still smiling up at me. "I didn't throw that bottle. I had nothing to do with it." Well, except driving the getaway car.

"Right." As she turned away, she gave me a last triumphant look over her shoulder. "Good luck with your campaign. Hopefully from now on you'll be able to convince your followers to keep their pants up."

And that was just the start of the day. By lunchtime I'd heard several versions of my wild night with Rich, Brett, and Shane. In some of them I was drunk, in some I mooned people. In all of them I had hauled my party guests over to Wilson's house in an attempt to vandalize the place.

Charity and Raine, I would like to add, didn't figure anywhere in these stories. Don't get me wrong, I'm glad their names weren't dragged down with mine into the tawdry world of drinking/mooning/vandalizing, but still I wondered why.

Was it because they were so good no one would believe they'd been involved with all of that, but me—the Frog Avenger—well, it was easy to think that I'd been doing all three things simultaneously?

Or maybe someone had it out for me. And if so, who? Jesse and Luke were the only ones that knew about the whole mooning thing. Luke might have told Bridget about it—that is, if he had managed to peel her away from Jesse's side for long enough to have a conversation with her. Could Jesse be the one who told Bridget all those outrageous stories?

The thought made my heart thud into my rib cage.

When I walked into English class, Wilson was sitting on a girl's desk at the front of the room fulfilling his daily quota of flirting. He ignored me, as usual, which for once I appreciated. I dropped my books on my desk with a thud and slid into my seat. Bill glanced over at me and nodded a hello, then went back to working on his homework. Jesse leaned back in his chair, watching me, and in his slowest drawl, said, "So are you talking to me today, or are you still pretending you can't see me?"

I had the urge to gaze past him and mutter, "Bill, did you hear something?" Instead I glared at Jesse. "I see you."

The muscles flexed in his jaw, making him look suddenly dangerous. "Good. Because I want to hear the explanation from your own lips. What were you doing riding around with a bunch of hoodlums Saturday night, and why were you chucking things at Wilson's house? Was that your idea of revenge or something?"

I leaned around Bill to get a better view of Jesse. "If I

wanted to take revenge on Wilson, don't you think I could come up with a better plan than, say, throwing an empty bottle at his driveway?"

Jesse leaned toward my desk, his blue eyes smoldering. "I don't know. Nothing you do makes sense anymore."

"Nothing I do? When did you drag your attention away from Bridget long enough to pay attention to anything I've done?"

Bill put his book down on his desk. "Do you want to switch places with me? I'll let you have my seat."

"I pay attention to what you're doing," Jesse said. "And the last thing I noticed you doing was driving around like a maniac while three guys made butt-prints on the car windows. I noticed that, Giovanna."

The mention stung, and I felt my face flush. "Yeah, while we're talking about Saturday night, who told the entire student body the mooning story?"

"I didn't tell anyone."

Bill's gaze swung to Jesse and then to me. "You know, they have counselors to help people work through these things."

I leaned over until I was touching Bill's desk. "Well, only you and Luke saw the mooning, but bright and early this morning Bridget was sure to rub it in. She must have found out somehow."

"And so you just assume it was me and not Luke."

Bill tapped his fingers against his desk and looked straight ahead. "Conflict resolution. That's what they call it. They probably have a twelve-step program or something."

"Yeah, I assume you told Bridget. She's been standing so close to you she can probably hear your neurons fire, let alone listen to every word you speak."

There was a glint of a smile in Jesse's eyes, as though he'd won a point of contention. "You keep bringing up Bridget. Why is that?"

I shrugged. "Would you like the long or the abridged version of all the things that are wrong with her?"

More tapping from Bill's desk. "Maybe it's not too late to transfer into World History. Of course, I'll be behind, and probably have to do hours of homework to catch up, but that's a small price to pay."

Jesse's expression turned serious. I couldn't have pulled my gaze away if I'd tried. In a lower voice he said, "The only one I told about last night was Wilson, and that's because I thought he had a right to know who was flinging things at his house."

"Then Wilson sure told a lot of people." Which, I realized as soon as I said it, was the truth. Of course Wilson had told everyone. I'd given him the perfect ammunition to use against Dante.

I glanced over at Wilson. He was now talking with two

girls up in the front of the room and smiling at both simultaneously. He'd come off as the victim in this whole affair, while Dante and I looked like some low-class thugs who used mooning drunks to vandalize his opponent's party.

Mrs. Pembroke stood up from her desk carrying a piece of paper. She raised one hand to get our attention, and the individual conversations among the students died away. "Well, class, I received another rejection letter."

She held up the paper for our examination, then walked over and stapled the letter to the bulletin board. I watched her numbly. Pretty soon she'd need more room. It takes a pretty big space to handle all of that rejection.

On the way to lunch I talked with Charity to find out how much trouble she'd gotten in. She said her parents understood, but she sighed a lot while she told me this, so I knew they hadn't been happy with her. "From now on I'm supposed to avoid the very appearance of evil," she said. "And I'm supposed to call them if anyone I know needs a ride home."

I didn't ask her if that whole appearance-of-evil thing applied to coming to my house. I mean, Gabby and Dante lived there, and both of them often appeared to be evil.

But hopefully the whole thing would blow over soon. Well, you know, after the kids at school stopped yelling, "Hey Giovanna, can you give me ride? I've got some stuff I want to throw at Wilson's house!"

At the end of the day Daphne drove me home. She talked cheerfully about her summer plans, and I was happy to let her rattle on because it meant I didn't have to think of many upbeat responses. Just before she pulled into my driveway, she said, "I found you a date for Thursday night."

I stared at her, trying to figure out what she meant. Denying rumors had taken up such a large portion of my day that I'd completely forgotten about everything else.

"It wasn't easy, either," she went on. "First I had to slyly find out from Luke where Wilson is holding his campaign meetings. I'd hoped he would have some of them at the club, because that is so Wilson's style, but most of them are before school in the library. Well, you can't very well bring some hot A-list Swain guy to the library in the morning. That wouldn't work."

"Oh, right." The reference finally clicked, and I remembered our conversation about A-list people, and how I was supposed to pretend to be one—which at this point was obviously hopeless. "Thursday night?"

"Right. Wilson is taking everyone who worked on his campaign out to dinner at five thirty at La Comida Ranchera. You know, sort of a thank-you dinner before election day. Which means Jesse will be there." Her voice was thick with implications. "Which means you should stroll in with Buddy around about five forty-five."

"Buddy?"

"That's just his nickname, because he's a really good singer and likes to sing Buddy Holly songs. Actually his name is Horton—and I know, that sounds like a geeky name, but he's named after his daddy. It's one of those family names that goes back for so many generations you're required to stick it on one of your kids." She shot me a conspiratorial smile. "But don't worry, he's gorgeous. Absolutely guaranteed to make any ex-boyfriend swell with jealousy."

I shifted my backpack on my lap so I was half hugging it. "You found a date for me? You did that already?"

She shrugged. "I know—I'm amazing. I had planned on waiting a little while—until the whole pool table thing blew over, but then after Raine told me about Saturday night, well, I figured it was only going to get harder to find you a man. So I called up Buddy Remington and explained the situation to him. It took a little begging on my part, but he finally agreed to play the part of the studly new rival."

"You told him all of it? He knows I'm just using him to make Jesse jealous?"

She blinked at me. "Well, I had to tell him."

I didn't want to imagine that conversation and how utterly pathetic I had sounded in it.

Daphne: Hi, Buddy, I have this friend who I'm trying to set up—

Buddy: I'm busy that night.

Daphne: I haven't told you what night.

Buddy: If she's not capable of getting a date on her own, then I'm busy.

Daphne (*because Daphne is delusional when it comes to her friends*): Giovanna is gorgeous, smart, and nice—everything anyone would want, but, well, she sort of has this criminal past, and there have been a few incidents lately where she appeared to be partially insane, but we're trying to find someone who'll make her ex-boyfriend jealous.

Buddy: Guess what—I'm still busy.

Daphne: I'll pay you.

I was just imagining the monetary negotiations when Daphne broke into my thoughts. "We'll get your hair done and go clothes shopping sometime beforehand, okay?"

"Okay," I said, because you can't turn down a friend who pays large sums to guys in order to get them to take you out. I trudged into my house, fingering my hair, and wondered how I had gotten myself into this.

I mean, Jesse and I had just fought. Again. I really didn't think that if I showed up with a guy, no matter how studly, it was going to make Jesse want me back. More likely Jesse would walk up to Buddy and offer him condolences.

But somehow I still had a date with a guy, a scenario to act out, and a pending haircut.

I mulled it over in my mind, looking for an excuse to

cancel, or the conviction to see it through. On one hand, Charity had told me I should talk with Jesse. But then Charity had never gone out on a date. Not even once. The guy she currently liked was my brother—which meant right off there was something wrong with her reasoning ability. Plus, Dante had no clue she liked him, which really didn't encourage me to trust her methods when it came to guys.

Daphne, on the other hand, thought I should show up with Buddy and this would help me get Jesse back. She'd been out with the equivalent of a small platoon and had men dangling from her fingertips.

So probably I should trust Daphne about this.

I walked inside and dialed my grandmother's number to set up a time to go to her house on Thursday. It wouldn't be too hard to convince Dad and Gabby to let me go. Thursday's not a big date night, so it shouldn't even raise their suspicions. Grandma didn't answer—a lot of times she takes naps during the middle of the day and turns off the phone—so I left a message. I waited for her to call back, but while I did, I kept hearing Jesse's voice in my mind saying, "You know Daphne's judgment isn't the best."

Chapter

13

Maybe Dante is right about me. I'm too emotional, and when I'm upset, I overreact and then regret it later. When Grandma called back after dinner, she asked me, "How was your day?"

I thought about the rumors, and how Wilson was bound to win the election, and how Jesse and I had fought in English, and with the phone still pressed to my cheek, I burst into tears.

Grandma said, "*Bellissima,* what's wrong? It's that woman again, isn't it? What has she done now?"

And then I had to tell her that no, surprisingly it wasn't Gabby this time. I didn't want to tell my grandma about the whole mooning incident, or that her grandson wasn't popular enough to win the school election, so I told her I felt awful because I'd broken up with Jesse. All my dates since then had been horrible, and I was obviously destined to end up as one of those old spinsters who lived with twenty cats and did crossword puzzles all day. Also I'd just realized that Dante was right about me, and I was way too emotional, but I couldn't help it, and how could I go to school tomorrow knowing I was too emotional, and I would probably do something to humiliate myself in English class?

Then Grandma spent the next half an hour telling me how wonderful I was and that Jesse didn't deserve me, and I wasn't too emotional, I was *piena di vita!* Grandma had been the exact same way as a girl.

I'm not sure how comforting that last part was, because it made me worry that I was doomed to be the kind of little old lady who insults her granddaughter's dates twelve seconds after meeting them. So you know, maybe there really is a time and place to rein in those overreactions.

Still, Grandma said I could come over Thursday night and in fact any night I ever wanted to, and she was going to invite over Gary, that nice young man from her bingo group, to meet me sometime.

"You don't have to," I said. "Daphne is doing a fine job of setting me up. In fact she's setting me up more than I want to be set up."

"But who is she finding for you? Is he Italian, this boy?"

"Buddy's American, Grandma. We're all American."

"Is he Catholic at least?"

If I had been smart I would have said, "Yes." I mean, what would it have mattered? The guy was already pretending to like me for Jesse's sake. What difference would it have made for him to be Catholic for one night? But instead I said, "I don't know," which earned me a lecture that I couldn't quite follow because she kept lapsing into Italian. Finally she said, "*Bellissima,* it will all work out for the best, and I'll see you on Thursday."

The next morning I felt a little better. I told myself that from now on instead of being emotional, I was going to approach my problems from a logical point of view. Dante obviously did this, and it worked well, because thus far he'd never been arrested. Well, okay, maybe he wasn't approaching the whole thing with Raine very logically, even though I told him again that she didn't like him. Dante wouldn't look at her, and he was clearly avoiding her.

I mean, really, was that the best way to handle things? He was going to hide from Raine until he was convinced she didn't like him anymore? Wouldn't the logical thing have been to talk to her and say something like, "Hey, I just like you as a friend"? And in which case she would have told him, "Hey, you're so full of yourself. What makes you think I like you in the first place?"

And then he would tell her about our conversation on Saturday, and well . . . maybe it was better for Charity if I let Dante be illogical about this one. I didn't want him to start avoiding her.

Anyway, the point is, I was trying not to be emotional. I examined the facts surrounding my problem. Fact 1) I broke up with Jesse because he'd betrayed Dante. Fact 2) That might have been an overreaction, but now we weren't on the best of terms, and Jesse had said some things that irritated me, but Fact 3) I had probably also said some things that had bothered him, like when I yelled, "We're through" in a roomful of people. Fact 4) Daphne had assured us that she knew the way to the concert stadium in Houston, but instead had driven us everywhere except to the concert stadium in Houston, so probably I should give Charity's advice a try and talk to Jesse.

So drawing upon the vast powers of logic, which, after all, were used to build complex things like computers, bridges, and an entire amusement park made out of Legos, I decided I needed to talk to Jesse. Face to face. These really weren't things I wanted to talk about over the phone. I didn't have time during English class, since I knew if I even looked in Jesse's direction, Bill would start into a treatise on transferring into World History.

But I had a good idea where Jesse would be in the morning. Daphne had said Wilson held his campaign meetings in the library. I'd seen Wilson hang out in the library before, so I knew where he liked to go—the very back corner of the nonfiction section. If I got there early enough, I could intercept Jesse before his meeting. I'd be casually reading up on the life of Nikola Tesla, and see him, and I'd say something like, "We really should talk."

And then we could work things out. Or he would tell me we couldn't work things out. In which case I was so going to La Comida Ranchera with Buddy to make him jealous.

Oops, I'd let emotion creep back into my thoughts. I had to stop doing that.

At breakfast time I sat down beside Skipper and Dante and poured myself cereal.

Skipper chomped on a spoonful of Cheerios, then tilted her head at me. "How come your eyes are puffy?"

Leave it to the five-year-old to notice details the adults overlooked. "I guess I'm having a reaction to my new mascara," I said.

Dante looked over at me but didn't comment.

Skipper kept staring. "Can I have it then?"

Skipper loves putting on makeup, with or without permission. "I wouldn't want it to make your eyes puffy," I said.

"Oh." She went back to eating her Cheerios, clearly disappointed by this outcome and probably scheming to get into my makeup as soon as I walked out the door.

Dante looked over at me again. "Is it that Jesse brand of mascara you've been using?"

I didn't answer him. "Can you drive me to school about a half an hour early?"

He glanced at the clock, then at his bowl full of cereal. "Why so early?"

I shrugged. "No reason."

"I won't be ready that soon."

"All right." I took another bite of my cereal. "I'll wait for Raine then. She mentioned she would stop by our house and offer us both a ride to school."

Dante held up one hand and shoveled cereal into his mouth. "Five minutes," he sputtered between mouthfuls. "Give me five."

You see, when used in the right way, logic can be a very effective tool.

When I walked into the library, no one else was there. This was because Dante had become so eager to leave the house before Raine supposedly showed up that he practically dragged me out the door on the spot. When he got to the school, he hurried off, I wasn't sure to where. Maybe he planned on hiding out in the boys' bathroom until school started or something. It made me feel a little guilty, but not guilty enough that I wanted to tell him the truth.

I went to the library, parked myself behind the biography shelf, and pulled out a book on Galileo. As soon as Jesse walked through the library doors, I would come out of my spot. I tried to go over casual opening lines in my mind.

Except what if he noticed my puffy eyes? I mean, I couldn't count on all guys to be less observant than my five-year-old sister. Maybe I should wait until another day when I didn't look like I'd spent last night crying. I could get Dante to take me early again if I mentioned Raine was stopping by tomorrow morning too. In fact, who knew how much stuff I could get Dante to do for me simply to avoid my friend? I may have stumbled upon the mother lode of motivators.

I peered at my reflection on the metal book shelf, trying to tell how bad my eyes looked. That's when I noticed Wilson and Luke walk in. They walked toward the back of the room, but Alex McCarthy intercepted them halfway there. Alex is the type of guy I'm well acquainted with, because I spent thirty days in the alternative learning center with people just like him. If he wasn't currently in trouble with the law, he'd be there soon. I wouldn't have thought much about Wilson stopping to talk to him, because Wilson in campaign mode talked to everybody, but Alex was a senior. Seniors couldn't vote. So Alex wouldn't have anything to say to Wilson about the election, and Wilson had no reason to try and win his vote.

While I watched, Wilson pulled his wallet from his

pocket, took out some bills, and handed them to Alex. Alex tucked them into his jeans, then without an acknowledgment or good-bye, he turned and strode out the library door. The whole thing happened so quickly that a moment later I asked myself if I'd really seen it. But I had, and I had no idea what it meant. Why would the mayor's son give someone like Alex McCarthy money? It seemed so sinister.

Wilson and Luke sat down at the table directly in front of my bookshelf. Instead of waiting for anyone else, they talked about Wilson's speech for the election assembly on Friday, and what he should and shouldn't say to the student body.

I gazed past them at the doors. I should have taken into consideration that Jesse probably wouldn't be the first one to come to the meeting. Now it would be awkward to walk out when he came. It would seem like I'd been spying on their meeting. Which I totally wasn't because, really, the talk was boring even in outline form.

Another thing I hadn't considered: What if Jesse walked in with Bridget? I couldn't tell him I wanted to talk to him with her standing right there.

Apparently this logic stuff took some practice, and I had failed miserably at my first attempt.

Wilson and Luke went on, and no one else came. I

couldn't walk out of the library unless I walked right past them. Which meant I was stuck here until they left. So I listened to them, because that was slightly more interesting than reading about where Galileo was born.

Wilson wondered if he should emphasize the dependability factor more blah blah blah, because he could get the job done better than Dante blah blah blah.

I was about to opt for Galileo after all when Luke said, "Dude, you've way overworked this campaign. You could have won without doing half the stuff you've done."

Wilson's grip on his paper tensed. "But people love an underdog, and in this election Dante is David and I'm Goliath. More than a few people would love to see me crash face-first into the dirt." He laid his speech back on the table, smoothing it out where he'd gripped it too hard. "Besides, if I lose, my dad will never let me live it down. He controls the whole city, and I couldn't win a stupid school election? It would be less humiliating to come home and tell him I want to enroll in ballet school."

Luke smirked at him. "Maybe, but think how spiffy you'd look in tights."

Wilson smacked Luke across the shoulder, and I ducked farther behind a row of books in case one of them looked in my direction. I couldn't see them anymore, but I still heard their voices.

"Just leave Dante alone," Luke said. "He's doing a fine job of driving away voters with stupid stunts like he pulled last Saturday. Come this Friday he'll have the word 'Loser' stamped on his forehead for good."

Wilson let out a sigh. "Should I put that joke about financing our ten-year reunion into my speech, or is that too much?"

"You know what you need to win by a landslide? Just don't ask anyone to prom before Friday. You've got every dateless girl in school voting for you."

Wilson gave a laugh that was almost a snort. "That's not what I have to worry about. What I have to worry about is how many of them will ask me to prom before the election."

Luke's voice lost its serious edge. "Man, they were all over you on Saturday. I nearly had to issue them numbers and make them stand in line."

"You think I should tone it down?"

"Nah, keep it up and let them all ask you to prom. In fact, turn the whole thing into a bidding war. Whoever offers the best deal gets you as their date." They both laughed at this, and then Luke added, "Low-cut dress and limo required."

"What will I do with the rest of my offers?"

"Keep one as a backup and cut the others loose."

More laughter. I peeked over the books and saw Wilson leaning forward in his chair. "No, I'll write them rejection letters like Mrs. Pembroke's."

"For their own personal bulletin boards," Luke said.

Wilson ripped a page of paper out of his notebook and placed it in front of him. "Dear Prom applicant . . ." He didn't say anything else, but whatever he wrote must have been funny, because Luke laughed so hard the librarian sent them one of those You'd-better-be-quiet-or-I'll-smack-you-with-your-own-book sorts of looks.

After that they laughed more quietly, but Wilson kept writing. I craned my head, trying to catch a glimpse of his words, but I was too far away. Then Luke glanced toward the front of the library. "Ditch the letter. Here comes Bridget."

I looked and then took a step over to where the books completely hid me. It wasn't just Bridget.

"It doesn't matter," Wilson said, but he crumpled up the paper anyway. "She's the only girl in school who doesn't want me to ask her." I heard the thud of paper hitting metal, and then Wilson said with forced lightness, "Two points."

"Bridget's just ticked off that you're flirting with other girls, so she's trying to make you jealous," Luke said. "That's the only reason she hangs off of Jesse like she was some kind of a Christmas tree ornament."

A moment later I heard them all say hello to each other—Bridget, Stacey, and Mr. Christmas Tree himself.

"Sorry we're late," Jesse said. "We passed out the rest of the 'Vote for Wilson' buttons."

"We didn't think you'd miss us," Bridget said, and I could tell there was another meaning to her words.

Wilson answered her unemotionally. "We didn't. We were going over my speech."

Was Luke right about her? And how would Jesse feel when he found out she only trailed around him to make Wilson jealous? I smiled, despite myself.

Wilson gave them a rundown of his speech—still just as boring—and then the bell rang. I heard them pick up their books and move their chairs. I listened as their voices and footsteps grew distant. And even then I didn't come out of my hiding place. I waited another minute until I knew they weren't coming back. Then I walked over to the garbage can, sorted through the trash, and pulled out a wadded piece of paper with Wilson's handwriting.

Dear Prom applicant,

Thank you for your interest and for throwing yourself at me, multiple times, like some love starved stork during mating season. After careful consideration of your work, I have decided that your face, body, and in all probability your ugly dress,

don't meet my current Prom needs. We wish you all
the luck in securing a date with some poor slob.
    Yours truly,
    Wilson Montgomery jr.

Maybe it wasn't the logical thing to do. I mean, I'd been trying to stay out of trouble with the school since last semester's suspension. But as I walked out of the library, I stole a roll of tape from the librarian's desk. I didn't even look back to see if she'd seen me do it. I grabbed it and kept walking.

You see, it's just so easy to fall back into your criminal ways once you've done suspension time.

Instead of going to trig, I waited until all the girls in PE class had dressed down and gone out to the gym, then I walked into the locker room. Right in the middle of the mirror, where every girl was bound to see it, I taped up Wilson's rejection letter.

I got a tardy slip for first period. But it was worth it. I mean, seriously, I smiled all through the lecture on inverse sine and cosine because I knew what was coming.

And it came. It came in a big way.

By the end of second period I heard snippets in the hallway. Girls talking about Wilson. "Did he really write that?"

"It was in his handwriting."

"What an absolutely conceited pig."

"I hope whoever he asks to prom turns him down."

By the end of third period the girls started a new election trend. They'd taken their "Vote for Wilson" buttons and drawn a red circle and a big slash across the words.

At lunchtime no less than five girls came up to me and asked who Dante was taking to prom. They all volunteered to go with him. I said I'd tell him, but to tell you the truth, I couldn't get near him. Everywhere he went, girls surrounded him. Wilson backlash had firmly set in.

And it was gratifying, really, to see the bewildered look on Wilson's face as he ate lunch. Luke, Jesse, Bridget, and Stacey tried to do damage control. Luke swore up and down that Wilson hadn't written the letter. He claimed it had been a frame job. But that's the disadvantage of having really distinctive handwriting, and then using it on your election posters.

Everyone knew he'd done it.

When I sat down in English class, I went out of my way to give Jesse a big, friendly hello.

He let out a sigh, and shook his head sullenly. "Don't say it."

"Don't say what?" I asked.

"Whatever it is you're planning to say, because I don't want to hear it."

So basically it wasn't a good time to bring up the we-need-to-talk discussion. It might have helped if I'd been able to wipe the so-Dante-doesn't-stand-a-chance-huh? smile off my face, but really, there wasn't much possibility of that.

When I went to PE class fifth period, the letter was still there, but all along its borders girls had scribbled in angry comments. Many of them the four-letter variety.

Yeah, someone would be eating their footwear soon, but it wouldn't be me.

14

The next day I had Dante bring me to school early again. I'd had enough time to get the happiness and basic gloating out of my system, and wanted to try to talk to Jesse again. Instead of going into the library this time, I hung out at the water fountain en route to the library, hoping to intercept him before he got there. But I didn't ever see him. I did notice that someone—not me, though I wished I'd thought of it—had taken Wilson's rejection letter off of the mirror and taped it onto the front of his locker.

I'm sure it gave the authors of those comments a lot of satisfaction to know Wilson could now read what they thought of his rejection letter, and I wondered if Mrs. Pembroke might try something along the same lines. I didn't suggest it, though.

In English class I smiled at Jesse in my old, flirty manner. "Hey, Cowboy."

"I still don't want to hear it," he said.

"Hear what?"

"Whatever it is you're dying to say to me."

"What if I'm just being friendly? What if I'm shooting the breeze?"

He watched me for a moment with narrow eyes, then turned back forward. "Nope, you're smiling too big."

"But—"

Bill leaned over toward me. "He doesn't want to talk, Giovanna. Respect his wishes."

Jesse let out a grunt and stretched his legs underneath his desk. "She didn't respect my wishes when she was my girlfriend. You expect her to do it now?"

I leaned over until my elbows rested on Bill's desk. "What's that supposed to mean?"

"You know what it means," Jesse said.

"No, I don't."

Bill slapped his hands down on his desk. "What is the deal with you two? Even when you're not speaking, you can't stop speaking to each other."

"Tell me what you mean," I said to Jesse, "because I always remember respecting your wishes."

Jesse's expression turned hard. "You didn't trust me about Wilson's campaign. I told you I had good reasons for supporting Wilson, but you wouldn't believe me."

"I believed you. I just thought you were wrong."

"You should have trusted me."

"Why? Because Wilson turned out to be such a stellar candidate? Mr. 'I'm too good to go with anybody to prom'?"

Bill raked a hand through his hair. "Haven't you all ever heard of the silent treatment? Maybe you should give it a try."

Jesse's eyes narrowed again. He shook his head as though trying to figure something out. "Tell me, Giovanna, how did that letter of Wilson's make its way to the girls' locker room?"

I shrugged. "Why ask me?"

"Because the day it happened, I thought I saw you in the library. For a second as I walked in, I thought I saw your face through one of the shelves."

A shiver ran down my back. My breath caught in my throat. I had to remind myself I hadn't really done anything wrong. Wilson wrote the letter; I'd just made it public. I forced myself to smile at Jesse. "That's so sweet. You see my face everywhere you go."

He nodded his head slowly, letting his gaze penetrate into my eyes. I knew, even though he didn't come out and say it, that he'd figured out the truth.

The heat of a blush spread across my face, and I hated myself for being so transparent. "Are you really going to defend Wilson for what he did?"

Jesse's voice took on an edge. "I don't know. It seems

like I've been so busy defending you lately that I'm not sure how much time I have left over to defend Wilson."

His words made me do a double take. "When have you ever defended me?"

He paused, and when he spoke again, his voice was quieter but his gaze just as penetrating. "I defend you every time I hear somebody talk about how you went joyriding around with Rich, Shane, and Brett, and every time I hear how no one should expect more from someone who burglarized the biology room."

My blush deepened. I sat stunned and silent as my mind shifted Jesse from the category of rival to defender. I wanted to thank him, to tell him exactly how I felt about everything, but even if I'd been able to conjure up the right words, I couldn't have said them here in the middle of English class. So all that escaped my lips was an inadequate, "Oh."

Then Mrs. Pembroke stood up and began her lecture. I turned away from Jesse, I had to, but even though I watched Mrs. Pembroke, I didn't hear a word she said. My emotions ping-ponged around my insides, and I thought of all the things I wished I had said to Jesse.

I tried again the next day—tried to find a time when I could talk to Jesse. I only saw him once outside of English class. He passed me in the hallway, walking alone, but when I said hi, he only nodded curtly at me and walked on. In English class he sat silently gripping his pencil with one hand and made a fist in his lap with the other. He never looked at me.

I sat miserably in my chair, wishing he'd say something, wishing I'd never gotten involved in this election, and basically developing a resentment of democracy altogether.

If only we had lived in a country ruled by some hostile dictator, none of this would have happened.

I kept glancing at him until the bell rang. Was he completely over me now? The thought made my throat ache.

After school Daphne picked me up and took me to her hairdresser to have him "shape" my hair. This involved cutting layers into it, and to tell you the truth, I panicked when I saw strips of my hair falling to the floor. I kept thinking about our short-lived career as musicians, and why in the world had I let Daphne talk me into cutting my hair? I'd probably end up looking like I was wearing an angry porcupine on my head, and far from wanting me back, Jesse would laugh himself silly when he saw me.

But then the stylist blew my hair dry, and I realized I had been wrong to ever doubt Daphne, because my hair looked good. Really good. I'm not trying to brag here, I'm just saying that I'd had this hair for seventeen years and never knew it was capable of swishing around my shoulders in cascading waves that way.

We went to a couple of stores at the mall, and Daphne found me a gorgeous Armani silk blouse. Granted, it cost roughly the same price as a college education, but it fit great. Daphne kept murmuring inspirational advice to me as I paid for it. "Remember, you're beautiful, and beauty has a persuasive power all its own."

We left the mall, Daphne dropped me off at my house, and I tried to remember all of her mantras as I walked across my lawn. I was confident. I was beautiful. Men would bow to my name. Or if not bow, at least talk to me in English class again.

I opened the front door, and there in the living room, talking to Dante, was Jesse. He sat on the couch. Dante sat on a chair. Both fell silent as I came in the room.

"Oh, um, hi," I stuttered, which broke about fifteen of Daphne's instructions right off the bat. In an attempt to make up for it I swished the hair from my shoulders in what I hoped was an alluring manner.

"Hi," Jesse said.

"Is there something wrong with your neck?" Dante asked.

I glared at him. It's hard to be alluring in front of your brother. Then I turned to Jesse with my best smile. "What brings you here?"

Jesse and Dante glanced at each other, then at me. "We were just talking about motorcycle stuff," Dante said.

Jesse stood up. "Well, I'd better get going. I've got this dinner with—" He stopped speaking as his gaze rested on me. "You changed your hair."

I fingered the ends happily. He'd noticed. "Yeah, Daphne thought it would look cute this way. Do you like it?"

His eyes narrowed. "Are you just doing whatever Daphne tells you to do now?"

I lowered my hand. "You don't like it?"

"No, I like it."

"Then you think Daphne was right about it?"

"Yes. No." His words grew flustered. "I mean, you should only change your hair if you want to, not because Daphne told you to." He folded his arms, and his gaze ran over me again in a skeptical manner. "Is she still setting you up?"

I shrugged, trying to be playful. "Well, she was right about my hair." And hopefully she was right about how to get an ex-boyfriend back too. For example, I liked the way Jesse looked at me so intently, his eyes glowing, as if he wanted to say a lot more to me. That was good. Plus, he'd come over to talk to Dante—which must mean they were trying to mend their friendship.

Life was looking up.

Jesse glanced at Dante again, then back at me. I could see frustration pass across his expression, but I didn't know why it was there. He nodded at me slowly. "We should sit down and talk about things after the election."

I smiled at him again, this time less certain. "Right."

Maybe he wanted to work things out, but just couldn't do it now because Dante was here. Then again, maybe "We should talk about things" was one of those phrases like "I just want to be friends," which people said when they broke up but they didn't really mean.

Jesse looked at his watch. "Well, I should go. See you around." And that was it. Jesse left. So apparently my beauty didn't have as much persuasive power as Daphne thought.

Dante turned away from me and walked out of the room. I followed him into the family room in time to see him pick Skipper off of the coffee table and set her down on the couch. "No standing on the table, squirt."

"I was making some toast," she said.

Thank you very much, Rich, for teaching that trick to my little sister.

"Not on the table," Dante said. "If you want toast, you'll have to eat it in the kitchen."

"Okay." She got up and trotted after him to the kitchen.

I wandered in and leaned up against the countertop. "So, it was nice of Jesse to come over and talk to you."

"Yeah." Dante dropped a piece of bread into the toaster and didn't look at me.

"Is everything cool between you two now?"

He shrugged. "Yeah."

"Do you think you'll go back to being friends after the election?"

"Sure."

"Even if you lose?"

Dante let out a slow breath. He walked to the fridge and got out the butter. "Look, I've been thinking about it, and I don't know, maybe I don't want to be student body president after all. It's a lot of work—and for what? It's not like it matters."

I stared at him. I tried to use my psychic twin powers to figure out what in the world he was talking about. I mean, this, now? After all the work I'd put into his campaign—after making posters, flirting with freshman guys, being pulled over by the police, and posting Wilson's memoirs in the girls' locker room—after finally getting Dante to the point where he might win, he didn't want to be president anymore?

The toast popped. Dante put it on a plate and buttered it, unconcerned.

I folded my arms and tried to think about the situation logically. "Are you crazy?" I asked. "Have you absolutely lost your mind? Do you realize I broke up with my boyfriend over this election? Do you realize I nearly got arrested with three drunk guys because of it? Don't tell me now that you don't want to be president!"

He put the plate down in front of Skipper. "I ran for president to make Wilson sweat a little. I never thought I'd win. Now it looks like I might, and you know what? I really don't care what our class gift to the school is. Let Wilson worry about it. He actually wants the job."

My teeth clamped together so hard that it took effort to speak. "You told me you wouldn't flake out about this."

He shrugged and turned away from me with an unconcerned air. "Sorry to disappoint you, but I guess I'm not the presidential type. I think I'm going to resign tomorrow."

I was not going to eat my shoes. No, I was going to force-feed them to Dante, and I might not wait until the election results to do it. Then something clicked in my mind. Maybe it was logic, or maybe that twin bond had finally kicked in.

I took a step toward Dante. "Jesse said something to you about the election, didn't he?"

"We talked about our bikes."

Now I was more certain. "He said something to you that made you decide to quit the race."

"Yeah, he said he thought I might win." Dante pulled a glass out of the cupboard, flipped on the faucet, and held the glass in the stream of water. His dark eyes flickered to mine. "The thing about you, Giovanna, is you're all about principles—even when it's not for your own good—but you have to understand that not everybody is like that. I'm not." He switched off the water and walked the glass over to Skipper. "So I'll resign from the race during my speech. No big deal. Life goes on."

I wanted to hate him. I probably did for about thirty seconds, because thirty seconds was the length of time I believed his story. My brother wasn't unprincipled. Jesse had said something to make Dante quit. And I wanted to know what.

I got ready to go to Grandma Petrizzo's house, silently fuming about it. Was Wilson using some sort of coercion on Dante? Would Jesse be a part of that? Could he be? I was torn between wanting to cancel my date with Buddy so I could forget Jesse altogether, and going to the restaurant just so I could chuck food at Jesse and Wilson when I got there. If I walked up to Jesse during dinner and demanded to talk to him, would he tell me the truth?

I drove to Grandma's house and rang her doorbell. She greeted me in her customary housedress. It had almost become a uniform. She took my face in her hands and kissed me on both cheeks. "Who is this beautiful visitor, eh? Come in, come in."

I said my hello, gave a brief and artificially upbeat report on how I was doing, then dumped all of my stuff in the guest bedroom. With a sigh, I took my makeup and trudged into the bathroom. I had consigned myself to going through the motions of this date, but only because it was too late to call it off.

As I got ready, Grandma appeared in the doorway of the room. "You want something to eat before you go on your date?"

"No, we're going out to dinner."

"You never eat enough. Look at you, you're a skinny girl."

"I'm supposed to be skinny, Grandma. In America 'skinny' is a compliment."

Grandma rattled off some Italian and shook her head in a disapproving manner, then said, "I'm having tortellini if you change your mind. The homemade kind. Not like the stuff you buy in the store. That's nothing but *immondizia*." Then she shuffled off toward the kitchen.

I finished applying makeup, touched up my hair, changed into the Armani blouse, and then surveyed myself in the mirror. Perhaps it was too formal for a casual restaurant and I should just change back into my school clothes.

As I stood there deciding, the doorbell rang. How had it gotten to be five forty-five already?

"I'll get it," I yelled, then scanned the room. Where had

I kicked off my shoes? I found them back in the bedroom. I didn't hear Grandma going to the door, but I ran down the hallway, shoes in hand anyway. The less time she had talking with Buddy, the better.

I ran by the kitchen and saw why Grandma hadn't answered the door. She has a TV on her kitchen table that she watches while she eats. She also has a recliner across from the table, because it's more comfortable to relax after dinner that way. Only she wasn't relaxing, or eating, she was asleep in front of the TV, with a plate full of tortellini on her lap.

The kitchen clock read five thirty-five. No wonder it had seemed like the time had flown by. Buddy wasn't supposed to be here for another ten minutes.

I stood in front of the door, called out, "Just a second," then slipped my shoes on and opened the door.

It occurred to me when I saw Buddy that Daphne had assured me he was gorgeous. I began to wonder exactly what Daphne's criteria for gorgeous was.

Not to sound shallow or anything, but the whole point of this date was to make Jesse jealous. The guy standing in front of me was on the chunky side and could have used a trip to the dermatologist for his skin condition. I smiled at him anyway, because let's face it, Daphne had probably had a hard time finding someone to date me, and this was as gorgeous as she could get. "Hi, Buddy, come in. I'm Giovanna." The words tumbled out of my mouth awkwardly, but he didn't seem to notice. He just came inside.

"Giovanna, I've heard a lot about you."

Well, I hoped not. I gave a nervous laugh. "Let me assure you, most of it isn't true." I looked around for my purse and realized I'd left it in the guest bedroom. "I've got to grab my purse, but hey, if my grandma wakes up and comes to talk to you, you're Catholic."

His eyebrows drew together. "Right."

I went down the hallway before he could ask what I was talking about, because to tell you the truth, I didn't want to explain. When I came back, Buddy was peering through the kitchen doorway at Grandma. "Sometimes she dozes off," I said and took my jacket out of the hall closet.

"Oh, well, I wouldn't want to wake her."

You can say that again. "She knows we're going out, so I don't think we need to say good-bye."

He looked at me, a bit startled, and I wondered if in his family it was considered rude to leave one's grandma lying under a plateful of tortellini while one went out on a date. "She'll be fine. She lives alone and everything," I said, then because he still hadn't spoken, I added, "Are you ready to go to the restaurant?"

He shrugged and looked thoughtful for a moment. "Sure. We can do that."

We can do that? Daphne had told him the whole point of this date, hadn't she? I didn't ask, because I couldn't find a graceful way to say, "You realize this is all just pretend, right?" Instead I said, "Do you know where La Comida Ranchera is?"

"Yep. I've been there before."

"Good." I walked out the door, and he followed.

The conversation in the car was the generic type of thing. We covered the weather quite completely. He apologized for the dog hair on the car seats, which there was quite a lot of, because sometimes he took his dog with him to run errands. He even laughed and said, "I'm glad I didn't take him with me tonight."

Uh yeah, I guess so, seeing as guys don't usually bring their dogs along on blind dates. I mean, I hoped that hadn't been a hard decision for him. Gee, I'm about to go out to dinner with a girl I've never met before. Should I take the dog along or leave him home?

I really needed to talk to Daphne about her matchmaking criteria.

He asked me if I had a pet, and so I told him about our cat, which I'm pretty sure led a boring life compared to his dog since I never took the cat with me on dates.

Then we made it to the restaurant.

I slung my purse over my shoulder, took a deep breath, and tried to walk up to the restaurant confidently. About two steps from the door I wanted to call the whole thing off, because first of all, I was mad at Jesse. Second, Buddy would not make Jesse jealous, so I didn't even want him to see us together. And third, this was just a stupid idea, and if the last series of bad dates had taught me anything, it was that I shouldn't put my love life in Daphne's hands.

But I'd dragged Buddy down to La Comida Ranchera, and I didn't know how to tell him I'd changed my mind without insulting him. Also, as I stood at the restaurant door, it occurred to me that I didn't know what Daphne had told him about his part in making Jesse jealous. I hoped he didn't plan on acting affectionate or trying to hold my hand or anything. I tucked my hands into my jacket pockets just in case. "We don't have to make a big deal about being here in front of the kids from my high school."

His eyebrows knit together. I could tell he had no clue what I meant.

I tried to elaborate. "We don't have to act . . . you know . . . it's just a normal dinner, so we shouldn't be too . . . um . . . friendly."

He opened the door to the restaurant, and I followed him in. His eyebrows were still scrunched together in that questioning way. "So you're saying you have friends here, but you don't want to be friendly to them?"

He missed my point, but instead of trying to explain

I answered his question. "I wouldn't mind saying 'hi' to them if they notice us—which they totally don't have to. I mean, we don't have to draw attention to ourselves."

Hopefully they wouldn't see me, or if they did, they would ignore me. Later, if any of the popular kids ever asked who that chunky guy with the rash was, I could make up something. I'd tell them I'd gone out to dinner with the head of the PETA scholarship fund for amphibian rescue.

We walked into the restaurant lobby. "A table for two?" the hostess asked. We both nodded, and she led us into the dining room.

Wilson's group sat in the middle of the room around three tables that had been pushed together. Bridget immediately saw me, and she must have said something, because the next moment every head turned to stare at us.

"Are those your friends?" Buddy asked.

"Yeah," I said. I tried to look away, but Buddy walked over toward them.

Hello, where in my convoluted explanation of what was supposed to happen tonight did I ever tell him I wanted to walk over to their table? But I couldn't not follow him. I made my legs move in that direction, although my stomach stayed back at the hostess station.

"Hey, how are you all doing?" Buddy asked the group. Then and only then did he turn to look and see where I was.

"Hi, guys," I said.

"Hi, Giovanna." Jesse's gaze went back and forth between Buddy and me, questioningly, but without any hint of jealousy.

Buddy pointed to Jesse's Aggies T-shirt. The logo is a big T flanked by a smaller A and M on either side. "Don't tell me you're an Aggies fan. C'mon, no self-respecting college would have the same initials as a bank machine." Buddy laughed at his joke, but no one else did. He didn't seem to notice. "Makes you wonder if the students go in and demand money every day. Like they have to give their pin number to get into class." More laughter—all his own by the way, since everyone at the table looked at him blankly.

Okay, great. Besides the extra weight and the skin condition, my date had a bad sense of humor. I had suspected from the car ride over that he might have the personality of lint, but now I was absolutely certain. And I'd just brought him inside to meet people I knew. Great.

The hostess stepped over to the table. "Are you part of this group?"

"No," I said.

Wilson held out a hand to some empty chairs at one side of the table and smiled at me generously. His voice came out in smooth, benevolent ripples. "You can join us if you want. There aren't any hard feelings between us, are there?" It had only been a few hours since Jesse had talked to Dante, but I could tell Wilson already knew he'd won the election.

I glanced at Jesse, blushed, and said, "We don't want to intrude."

But Jesse wasn't about to let me get away that easily. "There's plenty of room," he insisted. "Sit down and introduce us to your friend."

I blushed, trapped. "Oh, this is Buddy." But right at the same time I spoke, Buddy went, "Hi, I'm Gary."

Then he sat down while everyone looked at me, because I'd just introduced my date by a different name than the one he'd given. Judging by their expressions, they were puzzled, but not nearly as puzzled as I was.

Gary?

I thought his name was Horton. Where did "Gary" come from?

I sat down in the seat next to Buddy/Gary/whoever while the hostess put menus in front of us and said she'd be back in a few minutes. Then I smiled at the group and tried to explain myself. "Buddy is a nickname."

Buddy/Gary/whoever laughed and shook his head. "One date and you're already giving me a nickname? I'd better think of one for you too then." He gazed at the ceiling. "What would fit you?"

This caused snickers from Stacey and Bridget's section

of the table. "I could help you think of a couple," Bridget said.

I forced another smile and flipped open my menu. "I wasn't giving you a nickname. Daphne told me you went by Buddy."

"Who's Daphne?" he asked.

Chapter

15

Let me say right now that there are many things you don't want to hear from your date while sitting in the middle of a restaurant. "Hey, look, the kitchen is on fire!" comes to mind. Or "Isn't that a giant, angry scorpion crawling across your shoulder?" would also be bad. But I think the very worst possible sentence I could have heard just then was, "Who's Daphne?"

If he didn't know Daphne, then he wasn't my date at all, and yet somehow, somehow I was stuck here with him anyway.

Well, if we wanted to be specific about the "somehow," it involved me opening my grandmother's front door, inviting this guy in, and then telling him to take me to a restaurant. He was probably just the meter reader, or the paperboy, or some sort of passing vagrant, and now we were eating dinner with my ex-boyfriend and his friends.

I gave a half-strangled laugh, which sounded like I was choking. The hostess came back and shoved a glass of water at me. I took a drink, because I didn't know what to say. I mean, how do you gracefully turn to your date and say, "Excuse me, but who the heck are you?"

And not only was I here with some strange guy, but worse yet, my real date had probably already come and gone to my grandmother's house. When no one answered the door, he would just naturally assume I'd stood him up. I bet after tonight my reputation with Swain guys would be so bad they'd hang warning posters about me in their cafeteria.

Gary-whoever-he-was took a slow sip of his water. "Your nickname has to be something that's forward, because you know, only a really forward woman asks a guy out three seconds after meeting him."

Bridget's voice rose to near laughter. "Giovanna asked you out? Now isn't that nice."

So, did I 'fess up to what I'd done, or pretend I'd overcome my shyness with strangers at the exact same moment I'd lost all taste in guys?

I couldn't decide. Either way I looked unforgivably stupid.

"How about Panther, because you're sleek and adventurous." Gary rose and lowered his eyebrows knowingly. "I admire a girl who's a risk taker, since I'm a risk taker myself." He picked up his menu and nodded as he scanned the contents. "It's all part of my thrill-seeking nature, I guess."

Everyone at the table stared at him, which was only slightly better than them staring at me for being newly dubbed "Panther." It was like everyone was just waiting to see what ridiculous thing he would say next.

If I suddenly faked a ruptured appendix, would Gary have to take me home—or was that one of those conditions you called an ambulance for?

Wilson and Luke exchanged a smile. "Thrill-seeking nature?" Wilson asked, and it was clear he didn't believe it. "So are you into bungee jumping or something?"

"No, I've got a weak stomach. I can't even do a tire swing without puking all over the place—and you just don't want to be around me after I've been on the Ferris wheel. Watch out below—if you know what I mean." He laughed and turned a page of his menu. "I'm talking about real thrills."

"Then you must ride a bike," Jesse said.

"Only when my mother doesn't let me drive her Hyundai, but I hate pedaling uphill."

An ambulance ride to the hospital wouldn't be so bad. I mean, okay, maybe the doctor and my parents would be mad when the X-rays came back normal and they figured out I'd faked the whole thing, but still, if I suddenly grabbed my side and rolled onto the floor moaning, Gary might stop talking. It would be worth it.

"So what do you mean?" Bridget asked. "What thrills a guy like you?" She smirked at me as she said this.

Oh yeah, this was all so amusing—me out on date with a total geek. It was awful, but on the bright side, I planned on ditching him as soon as possible. And since he was a stranger, I'd never have to see him again. I wouldn't even tell him my last name. He didn't know where I lived.

"High stakes poker," Gary said. "Blackjack. Roulette. Even bingo. That's where I know Giovanna's grandmother from. She and I are bingo buddies."

"Crap," I said.

He nodded. "I love craps too. Just can't get enough of the Las Vegas life. I'm going to move there soon—well, just as soon as I pay off my gambling debts, anyway."

"Gambling debts," I repeated.

"It's only a few thousand dollars. I could make more than that on a good day at the races, but my parents won't even let me try. They just don't understand building wealth. You've got to spend money to make money."

Jesse leaned back in his chair. "Actually, that phrase is about investing, not gambling."

Gary waved his hand as though to wipe away Jesse's words. "It's the same thing."

"No, gambling is more like taking all your money and giving it to the people who run casinos," Jesse said.

Gary shook his head. His lips twisted into a sneer. "You all are just too young to understand. You're only in high school."

Which side was an appendix on? I needed to know where I should grab before I started moaning in agony. This was clearly one of those areas where schools are failing today's kids, because no one had ever taught me this information. Maybe if I'd dissected that frog like I was supposed to I would have at least been able to tell you where a frog's spleen was located, but I had no idea where my own appendix was.

Luckily, before I'd decided to grab both sides, the waitress stepped up to our table. "You folks ready to order?"

We ordered, and for a few minutes the group talked amongst themselves. I prayed that Gary would just be quiet for a while. Funny how dating had turned me religious. The last time I prayed I was huddled under a pool table.

I took a drink of water and tried to remember whether there was a patron saint for bad dates. If there's not, there really should be.

Mostly I pretended to be absorbed in Bridget and Stacey's conversation, because then I didn't have to look at Gary, who kept trying to get my attention by saying things like, "Hey Panther, do you sing karaoke? I know a great karaoke bar. Maybe for our next date we could go there."

Jesse acted like he was listening to Luke and Wilson, but I could tell he heard every word Gary said. He had his elbow on the table and his hand resting against his mouth to try and cover his smirk.

The waitress brought our food, which I ate quickly, not because I was hungry, but because chewing gave me a built-in excuse not to talk to Gary. Unfortunately, eating didn't stop him from talking, often with his mouth full. He told me about the landscaping business he was trying to start up, which right now only consisted of mowing lawns, but he planned to work his way up to bushes and trees. That's what he'd been doing over at my grandmother's house. He'd come to see if she wanted someone to take care of her yard.

Gary spent several minutes talking about weed extermination, and the dangers of white flies, which is really just the thing you want to hear about while you're eating your chicken enchilada.

Only once did Gary stop talking to me. For a brief time he tried to explain his blackjack methodology to Jesse, which would one day make him fabulously wealthy.

In return, Jesse tried to explain that in gambling the odds are always against you, and Gary had a greater chance of being hit by a bus full of casino owners than he did of becoming fabulously wealthy by playing blackjack.

Then Gary turned back to me. "Once I make the big time, I'll send you a ticket so you can to come visit Vegas, Panther."

"You don't have to keep calling me Panther," I told him.

He wiggled his fork in my direction. "If I'm your Buddy, then you're my Panther."

"You're not my Buddy."

"Uh-oh. Panther has her claws out."

Normally, I would have just gone back to my enchilada and ignored him. You know, just ride it out and try to make the best of a bad situation. But Jesse sat across the table watching me with his time-stopping eyes. I didn't want him to think, for even one second, that I was any-body's Panther. So I unclamped my lips. "Look, Gary, just stop it."

"Her fur is raised. Next she's going to pounce. Cats always go for the neck, don't they?"

Jesse put one hand on the table and leaned toward Gary. Slowly, he said, "The lady told you to stop that."

Just like that, the rest of the conversation at the table halted. Gary didn't notice. He shrugged back at Jesse. "It's not any of your concern, now is it?"

Jesse's eyes flashed. "It is if I say it is."

I put my fork down. Suddenly I wanted nothing more than to flee from this restaurant. I couldn't look at Jesse. "I'm finished with dinner," I told Gary. "Are you ready to take me back to my grandmother's house?"

Gary grudgingly pulled his attention away from Jesse and held his hand up in the air. He snapped his fingers to get our waitress's attention. When she didn't look at him, he snapped louder. "I'll get you a doggy bag—or in this case a kitty bag."

The waitress finally turned toward Gary, and he yelled, "Can you bring us a doggy bag and the check?"

She nodded and left. I let out a sigh. It would all be over soon. I looked at my enchilada, my fork, the napkin on the table, anything but Jesse's disapproving eyes. The plan had been to make him jealous. Instead I had humiliated myself by showing up with a socially inept gambling addict.

Gary reached into his pants pocket and pulled out his wallet. He flipped it open and then shut it again. "Hey Panther, I hope you have some cash, because I'm low on funds."

The table grew silent. "What?" I asked.

"I don't have any money, but after all, you're the one who asked me out. You get the check this time, and I'll pay when we go out for karaoke."

Okay, I'd like to point out that even Dave, Mr. Circle-

K-Fudgsicles, didn't make me pay for his part of our date. And call me old-fashioned, but if Gary knew he had no money and was planning on sticking me with the check, should he really have ordered the expensive steak chimichanga platter?

I picked my purse up off of the floor, feeling every single stare sent in my direction. I knew I had a twenty-dollar bill in my wallet. I hoped I had more. My chicken enchilada cost about ten dollars. His dinner was more than that. We'd both only had water to drink, but I needed money for taxes and the tip. I flipped my wallet open. There was only the twenty. The picture of Andrew Jackson looked away from me forlornly, which was more than everyone else at the table did.

"Are you okay?" Stacey asked. "You look flushed."

I put my purse in my lap and tapped my fingers against the strap. "That may be because my appendix just ruptured."

"Nah, you'd be in more pain," Gary said.

"Oh, I am. I just hide it really well."

Bridget picked up her glass, and for a second I thought she was going to offer a toast. Instead she said, "Panther, you're such a kidder."

I turned away from her and looked at Gary. "Do you have any money at all? Because I only have a twenty."

He shook his head, unconcerned. "My parents cut up

my credit cards, but don't worry. We can always wash dishes to make up the difference. I've done it before."

Not in a silk Armani blouse, he hadn't.

I couldn't see another choice. I turned to Jesse. "Can you please lend me some money? I'll pay you back as soon as I get home."

A grin spread across his face. He stretched his shoulders, put his hands together, and cracked his knuckles. "I think we could work out a deal."

Great. He was about to tell me I had to do something terrible like wear a "Vote for Wilson" button tomorrow. My throat felt tight; still I said, "What did you have in mind?"

Jesse turned from me and looked over at Gary. "How would you like to make a little wager?"

Gary's eyebrows rose. "I don't usually make little wagers, but I can make an exception. What are you fixing to wager?"

"Your date," Jesse said.

"Me?" I asked.

Jesse nodded as though it were nothing. "You said you wanted to borrow money."

"But . . ." But you can't just wager people. This wasn't some medieval slave market where you could buy somebody. I didn't say any of that of course, because my common sense kicked in immediately after I said the word *but*. As I saw it, if Jesse wanted to wager me away from Gary—great. I was even willing to help him cheat in order to win.

"What's your game?" Gary asked. "I've got dice in my car."

"Something more simple than that. A number game."

The waitress walked up to our table and put a Styrofoam box down beside my plate. Before she could lay the billfold with the check onto the table, Jesse held his hand out for it. He laid it down in front of him without opening it. "If I win, then Giovanna is my date. I'll pay the bill, but you'll have to agree to leave and never contact her again."

"And if I win?" Gary asked.

"Then I'll pay your bill plus give you an extra ten you can use for dessert on the way home." Finally, Jesse turned to me. "Do you agree to the terms? I don't think you'll get a better offer, and I'd hate to see you in the kitchen scraping food off of plates."

"It's a deal," Gary said.

Jesse didn't look at him. His eyes stayed on me, waiting. His tone turned gentle. "Do you agree, Giovanna?"

"I agree," I said.

He smiled at me, and yes, time did stop. Then he turned to Gary. "On your check are several numbers." Jesse picked up the billfold and turned it around as though trying to see through the leather. "We could bet as to whether the total was even or odd. We could bet as to what all the digits added up together would equal, or—I know—we'll both pick a number between one and ten. Whoever is closest to . . ." He paused, then shrugged. "The last digit of the total before taxes wins. I'll let you pick first."

Gary smiled confidently. "A good gambler knows that in this game you always choose the number five. It gives you the best odds."

"Fine. You take five. I'll go with the number eight." Jesse handed the billfold to Gary. "Why don't you open it and tell us what the number is."

Gary chuckled and shook his head. "You've got a lot to learn about gambling. You should have chosen either four or six. Four would have let you win with any number lower than five. Six would make you a winner with any number higher than five. With eight your chances of winning are . . ." his voice trailed off as he opened the billfold. He stared at the check for a moment and let out a grunt.

"What's the number?" I asked.

Gary handed the bill to Jesse. His lips momentarily pursed. "Eight."

I tried not to smile too widely. "Well, Gary, it was nice meeting you and everything. Have a good drive home."

Gary let out a sigh, but nodded. "Right, thanks for dinner." He didn't look at me as he stood up and left the table. I almost felt sorry for him. He looked so sad as he plodded away.

When he was out of earshot, Luke said, "Well, that's how you know you've got a gambling problem. When you lose your girlfriend at dinner, it's time to call that one-eight-hundred number."

"I wasn't his girlfriend," I said.

Stacey smirked at me. "Whatever you say, Panther."

Bridget put both elbows on the table and leaned toward Jesse. "So was it a lucky guess, or did you somehow look at the check to see that the number was an eight?"

"I'm not a cheater," Jesse said. "But I'm not a gambler either. I just do math." He took out his wallet and counted out bills to put in with the check. "All the prices on the menu end in the number nine. Giovanna and Gary ordered two items. Two times nine is eighteen. Eighteen ends in eight. If Gary hadn't been so caught up in his gambling methods, he might have realized that."

Well, that was probably a kinder assessment of Gary than he deserved.

Chapter

16

After the bill was settled, Jesse and I left the restaurant. When we got to the parking lot, Jesse's paced slowed. With a teasing look he took hold of my hand. "I can do this because you're my date now." He gently squeezed my fingers. "I won you fair and square."

I let him hold my hand, in fact I squeezed his hand back, even though I knew this was disloyal to Dante. "Thanks for paying for my dinner, and, you know, saving me from Gary."

"I told you not to let Daphne set you up."

I hated to admit the truth, so I did it with a sigh. "This date wasn't Daphne's fault. It was all a big mistake and just bad luck. Really bad luck. In fact, I bet one of my ancestors defiled an Egyptian tomb or something."

Jesse laughed and pulled me a step closer to him. I

could smell the familiar scent of his cologne. It felt irresistibly like old times, and I wondered whether he wanted me back, or whether he was just enjoying the victory of winning me in a bet.

I took sly glances at his face but couldn't read anything from his expression. He looked happy and confident, but that might be because this was the punch line to my joke of a date.

"I guess I have a talent for making mistakes," I told him, and I hoped he understood that I wasn't just talking about Gary.

He took a few steps in silence, considering, then said, "Well, you were right about one thing. Remember when you criticized my friends?"

My heart jumped at his words. Even as the thought came to my mind, I dismissed it, but still I hoped that he'd found out the truth about Wilson. Maybe that was why he'd come over to talk to Dante. Maybe Jesse hadn't done anything to make Dante quit the race after all.

"Yes," I said.

"Well, Stacey and Bridget can get a might catty at times. Actually a lot of the time."

"And?" I didn't say Wilson's name then, but I thought it.

"And I thought you should know you were right. I guess

I never put my finger on it to begin with, but that's what I first liked about you. You weren't that way. You were always nice to everybody."

"Oh." Instead of making me feel better, his words stung. Did he still think this about me, even after what I'd done to Wilson? I didn't want to ask, and yet I had to say something. "About Wilson . . ." I didn't know how to say the rest of it, so the sentence drifted off.

He looked away from me, out across the darkness of the parking lot. "You were still wrong about Wilson. I mean, he invited you to sit with us tonight even though you're campaigning for his opponent. That's nice, isn't it?"

"I guess." Did this mean I was wrong about Jesse saying something on Wilson's behalf that made Dante decide to quit the campaign? Jesse wouldn't stand here defending Wilson if he knew Wilson was forcing Dante to quit, would he?

But there had been something—I was sure Dante wouldn't flake out about this. Not now. The whole thing twirled around in my mind, unraveling into a jumble.

We came to Jesse's bike, but neither of us climbed on. I held onto Jesse's hand, but more loosely now. "After you left our house today, Dante said he didn't want to be president anymore."

"Did he?" Jesse voice was low and smooth, without any hint of surprise. It was as good as an admission of guilt.

"What did you say to him?"

"We talked about our bikes."

"Okay, I didn't believe that explanation when Dante gave it to me, and he's a better liar than you are."

Jesse reached out and slowly ran his finger across the length of my cheek. "You know, sometimes you've got to trust the people you love. You've got to trust that if they're good people, they'll make good decisions."

I didn't understand exactly what Jesse meant, but this might have been because he was standing so close. He still had his hand on my face, and now he leaned down, looking at my lips. "Do you trust me, Giovanna?"

I couldn't breathe. My heart doubled its pace. I didn't answer. He leaned even closer until his lips nearly brushed against mine. "Do you?" he asked.

"Yes," I said.

He kissed me, and I wrapped my arms around his neck. I did trust him at that moment—and the next moment. I trusted him until several minutes later when he released me. Then he ran his hand through his hair and said, "I guess I'd better get you home."

That was it? He wasn't going to offer any explanation?

"Wait," I said. "What about Dante? What about all of that stuff you said about trust?"

He shrugged. "I meant it." He climbed onto his bike and slipped his helmet in place as though the conversation was over.

I still didn't move. "What's that supposed to mean?"

"It means, trust me and trust Dante, and we'll talk about the rest of it later."

"You mean after the election? We'll talk about it after Dante throws the election?"

"Right," he said.

I climbed onto the back of Jesse's bike and put on the extra helmet he always carried with him. I wound my arms around his waist to hold on, but my insides went numb. I didn't feel like trusting him anymore, and I didn't want Wilson to win the election. As for Dante, I knew very well I'd betrayed him tonight by getting back together with Jesse. I'd betrayed my brother with a kiss.

I called Daphne when I got home and told her the news: the night had ended with Jesse and me embracing in the parking lot. Then I told her the other news: that I had accidentally stood up Buddy and gone out with a stranger. *Stranger* in this instance meaning both definitions of the word.

She said that she'd call Buddy and explain and then told me how happy she was that things had gone well with Jesse. She was probably just happy that she could exit the doomed carnival ride that was my love life, but still, she was happy.

The next morning Gabby fussed over Dante before we

left for school. Did he have his speech? Didn't he think he should wear a nicer shirt to stand up in front of the student body? How about the one Grandma Petrizzo had given him last Christmas?

After Dante assured her that he was completely prepared and wouldn't touch Grandma Petrizzo's shirt even if it were lined with ten-dollar bills, she stopped bothering him. Still, as we walked out the door, she called after us, "It doesn't matter if you win or lose, Dante. We're still proud of you for trying your best."

I looked at Dante to see if he'd wince because he'd already decided to quit, but he smiled at her and waved good-bye.

How was it that no matter what he did, Gabby was always on his side? She never took my side, and despite what Dante said, all of the compliments in the world wouldn't change that.

I tried to talk to Dante on the way to school, which isn't the easiest to do on a motorcycle because they are as noisy as lawnmowers, plus your helmet muffles everything you say.

But at every stop sign I badgered him. "Is Wilson blackmailing you? Is that it?"

And Dante kept saying, "Would you just drop it?"

As soon as we got to school, he took off so he could rewrite his speech. Since I didn't have anything else to do,

I stood by Charity's locker, waiting for her and growing more frustrated at Dante for not telling me what was going on. She finally showed up and set her backpack down on the ground with a thud. "Hi, Giovanna."

"I still don't know what you see in him."

She flipped through her combination. "Who?"

As if she didn't know. "You've got to talk to him. He's resigning from the race."

Her hand stopped on her lock. "Why?"

"I don't know. He says he doesn't want to be president anymore, but I think Wilson blackmailed him."

She resumed turning her combination, this time more slowly. "What has Dante ever done that someone could blackmail him?"

"Who knows? Maybe he did something bad once."

Charity shook her head and opened her locker door. "If he had, he'd be the first one to announce it. He's so into that whole rebel image. The only thing he'd hide is season tickets to the symphony or a membership in the Audubon Society."

I hugged my books to my chest. "Well, it must have been something. Jesse came over to talk to him, and then suddenly Dante wanted to quit."

"Jesse?" Charity arranged books in her locker, putting some from her backpack in and taking others out for class.

"Jesse isn't the type who'd help Wilson blackmail some-body."

"Yeah, but Jesse also isn't the type who'd turn his back on Dante and work for Wilson in the first place, and yet he did. It's like Wilson has some secret power that's turned them all into election zombies."

Charity didn't answer, but Raine walked up to the two of us. "Who's a zombie?"

"Dante," Charity said.

Raine nodded. "I knew there was something wrong with him. Have either of you noticed that he doesn't finish his sentences anymore—and he always thinks he's supposed to be somewhere else? Every time I see him, he's darting off someplace."

Charity took out the last of her books and shut her locker. "He decided he didn't want to be president after all, so he's quitting."

Raine's mouth actually dropped open. "No sir," she said.

"Giovanna thinks I should talk to him, but I don't know what good that would do. He's never listened to me in his life."

"I'll talk to him," Raine said, her mouth set in a hard line. "He can't quit and make everyone who supported him look stupid. I went to his party. I told a roomful of guys I was dating someone from Swain named Thor. I bet that's why no one from our school has asked me to prom, and now he doesn't want to be president? I don't think so. He owes me a better explanation." She took several steps down the hall. "And he owes me a prom date too."

Charity and I both watched her go. We looked at each other, and then at Raine's back tromping down the hallway.

"Well, that should be an interesting conversation," I said.

"If she can find him," Charity said. "He does a pretty good job of avoiding her."

The two of us walked toward our first period classes, weaving in and out of other students. I fingered the books in my hand. "Maybe we should tell her the truth."

"No. And don't you dare tell Dante that I like him. I don't want him to start speaking to me in half sentences and telling me he has to be somewhere else."

We walked a few more steps in silence. "If you never find a way to tell him how you feel, he'll never know."

"That is the point," she said.

"Maybe he secretly likes you back."

"It's not meant to be. And when something isn't meant to be, you leave it alone."

Which didn't seem like an answer to me. I mean, how could she just decide it wasn't meant to be? I didn't press the issue, though, because I'd learned an important lesson from Daphne. Matchmaking is a lot harder than it looks.

During my morning classes I tried to use our twin bond to send Dante psychic messages not to resign. Whatever control Wilson had on him, he could fight it. Or better yet, he could outsmart Wilson. Wasn't that the way it always worked on TV? When the hero is presented with some awful choice—like the villain is going to blow up an orphanage if the hero doesn't give himself up to the villain's evil clutches—instead of turning himself in, the hero finds a way to save both the orphans and himself, plus he gets a really hot girlfriend by the time the ending credits roll by.

Dante had watched a lot of TV. He should know this.

At fourth period, the freshman, sophomore, and junior classes went into the auditorium to hear the candidates speak. I saw my friends sitting in the middle section of the bleachers. Dante and the rest of the candidates sat on folding chairs on the floor of the auditorium. They were lined up by position, with the people running for secretary closest to the podium. The presidential candidates sat the farthest away. Dante was at the very end of the line, the last to give his speech. He stared up into the crowd and looked so alone. For a minute I stood by the door watching him while the masses flowed past me on their way to the bleachers.

I couldn't let it happen. I mean, how could I just stand there and let Wilson take the election away from my brother?

I went to the side of the auditorium, picked up a stray chair, and walked over to Dante. After putting the chair beside him, I sat down.

"What are you doing?" he asked. "You can't be here."

"If you resign, I'm going to make a speech and tell everyone that Wilson blackmailed you, and they should vote for you anyway."

His jaw clenched and he shook his head. "No, Giovanna. Go sit with your friends."

I didn't move. I folded my arms and looked out into the crowd. A thousand people sat in the stands. Just seeing them all en masse made every part of me shrink, but I still didn't move.

Dante leaned toward me. "I know you're bluffing. When we moved here, you wouldn't even introduce yourself to anyone for a month. There is no way you're getting up in front of the entire school to say anything. Now please leave."

I could see Jesse sitting toward the front of the bleachers. He stared at me with questioning eyes. I pulled my gaze away from him and turned back to Dante. "If you don't want me to make a speech, then don't resign in yours. Otherwise, I'll walk to the podium right after you."

"You're bluffing," he said again, but he looked at my eyes more closely. After a moment he let out a sigh and a few swearwords.

Chalk one up for the twin mind-meld. I wasn't bluffing. Trembling, yes, scared to death, yes, but I wasn't bluffing.

Dante edged toward me on his chair. His eyes took on a look of resignation, and he lowered his voice to a whisper. "Look, Giovanna, this is the way it is. You know how you have that police record?"

I nodded. It's not something I ever forgot.

"Wilson told Jesse that if Jesse helped him win, Wilson could do something to have your name cleared. Do you understand everything now? When Wilson wins, you'll have a clean record. You can apply for any job you want and go to college anywhere." He turned and faced forward again. "So I'm resigning."

The buzzing of the crowd seemed to grow louder as everything that had happened over the last two weeks rearranged itself in my mind. I looked over to where Wilson sat talking with the vice-presidential hopefuls. What could he do that would clear my record? I wasn't sure, but somehow I didn't doubt for a minute that he could do it. Then I stared at Jesse in the audience. All along he'd been trying to help me. It made my breath catch in my throat.

"Why did Jesse wait until last night to tell you?"

"Because he didn't think I was going to win until last night. He didn't want to make me choose between running and helping you." Dante pointed up to the middle of the crowd. "Look, there's where your friends are sitting. They're saving you a place."

I still didn't move. My heart simultaneously felt so achingly full and so pierced that I couldn't believe it kept beating. I wanted to be free of that police record. Just the thought brought to mind a future I could jump headfirst into. All I had to say was, "Thanks, Dante. Go ahead and resign." He planned on doing it, after all. And my future was there, dangling within reach.

But I couldn't let it happen. I knew that.

For a moment I wished I had never brought this chair over and sat next to Dante, that I'd never forced him to tell me what he was doing. But I pushed those thoughts away and faced my brother. "Don't resign for me, Dante. This election is about you, not me."

Another swearword from Dante. He shut his eyes. "See, I knew you would say that. That's why we had to keep it a secret from you. Jesse and I both knew you'd try to be all noble about it."

"Well, you were right. I'd rather have you win."

He didn't say anything, just looked out at the crowd, then he shrugged. "Fine. It's your future. If you don't care about it, why should I?" He waved in the general direction of the audience. "Now would you go sit in the stands before you get me in trouble?"

"You're going to give your first speech?"

"Yes."

"Really?"

"Yes, now go. The principal's walking to the podium."

I stood up and hurried to the bleachers, crawling past people to sit in between Charity and Daphne.

Daphne leaned over to me. "Giving Dante a last minute pep talk?"

"Something like that," I said.

The principal gave a brief discourse about how blessed we were to live in a democratic society, then introduced the candidates. The people running for secretary, treasurer, and vice president spoke. They said the usual stuff. I promise I'll do a great job, and so on. They threw in little school spirit snippets to get the audience to clap—which everyone did, probably so their arms wouldn't fall asleep.

Finally Wilson strolled to the podium. He smiled up at everyone and no one in particular. While he spoke, polite applause and hoots of encouragement surrounded him. Then Dante stood up and walked to the podium. My heart followed his every footstep.

He stood in front of the microphone and set his speech

on the podium. I would have been shaking, but he looked up calmly. "First of all, I want to thank everybody who worked on my campaign, gathering signatures and making posters and stuff. Thanks for believing in me." He looked up toward me and smiled. A pause stretched through the auditorium, and then he spoke again. "But the more I thought about it, the more I realized I was running for president for the wrong reason."

No, this wasn't his first speech. I stared at Dante, shaking my head. Despite everything he'd said to me, he was resigning. I didn't know whether I wanted to yell at him or kiss him.

"The thing is," Dante went on, "I originally wanted to do some sort of memorial for Norman Pike, you know, just something that said our class remembered him. When the student council wouldn't do anything, I decided, no problem, I'd run for president." Dante put both hands on the podium, gripping it on either side. His gaze moved from the audience to the paper in front of him, but he wasn't reading. "Norman was one of us. We shouldn't forget him. We shouldn't overlook people. Not anybody."

Dante shrugged, and his attention went back to the audience. "Then I realized I don't have to be president to make a memorial happen. All I need is for you to help me show the student council that we want to do something for Norman." Another shrug, and Dante leaned in to the microphone as though to let us in on a secret. "I figure, why not let Wilson plan the dances, fund-raisers, and all that stuff. He wants to do it."

Dante took a step back, raised both hands up as though conducting an orchestra, and called out, "Let's tell the student council that we want a memorial. Put your hands together for Norman!"

The noise was immediate. It didn't trickle in, it didn't build, it filled the room fully formed. Clapping, stomping, and the chant, "Nor-man! Nor-man!" vibrated around me. I chanted myself, although I barely heard my own voice. The energy of the crowd swallowed it whole.

It didn't seem like defeat at all. Dante had turned his resignation into something powerful.

"Nor-man! Nor-man!"

I wished Norman could have heard his name booming through the auditorium. No matter what else we did, this was the memorial I would remember.

Finally Dante stepped back up to the microphone and called out, "Thank you! I think the candidates for student council heard us." He turned sideways, looking over to the chairs where the candidates sat. "Hey, can I see by a show of hands which of you pledge to work on a memorial for Norman if you're elected?"

They didn't hesitate. Every hand went up.

"Cool." Dante nodded and picked up his speech.

"That's all I really wanted to say, so I'm officially resigning. Thanks."

He walked back to his seat, and every gaze in the room followed him. Charity leaned toward me and over the noise of the clapping said, "That's what I see in him."

Even though Dante resigned, the race was still close. But this was only because someone started a write-in campaign, and the student body nearly elected Norman Pike as the posthumous school president.

I suppose it's a good thing he didn't win, though, because I doubt Norman would have been good at all the technical aspects of the job that, you know, required you to be alive. Still, it gave me an odd sense of satisfaction that Wilson nearly lost to a dead guy.

I knew I wouldn't see Jesse before school ended, so I texted him that I wanted to get together and talk. Then I compulsively checked my phone for an answer, which he never sent.

I tried to find a time to talk to Wilson about what he was going to do to clear my record, but that didn't happen until after school. And that was only because I ran into him at Dante's locker talking with my brother.

When I walked up, Dante was nodding his head, listening to Wilson with apparent approval.

"So it's all done then?" Dante asked.

"My father took the evidence in to the police chief last night."

"Last night?" Dante let out a grunt and raised one hand in the air. "What if I hadn't resigned today?"

"I knew you would." Then Wilson winked at me. "But if you hadn't, well, I guess I would have helped Giovanna anyway."

"Helped me how?" I asked. "What exactly did you do?"

Wilson gave me a wide grin. I knew it was just because he was happy with himself, but he really did have a nice smile. It was enough to make me forgive Raine for being so silly about him. "Well, a few weeks ago, I got to thinking about you and the whole biology break-in," Wilson said. "I always believed in your innocence. You had no reason to steal things. Tim Murphy, on the other hand—well, drug habits are expensive. I'm sure most of the stuff from the biology room went right to a pawn shop with anything else he'd stolen recently. But the computer had a serial number. A person can't just pawn those without the risk of being caught. Still, it was worth at least a thousand dollars secondhand, so it's not the kind of thing he'd get rid of either. I figured he was just waiting for an opportunity to unload it, and the best way to collect evidence of your innocence was to give him the opportunity."

Wilson paused, maybe for effect or maybe just to take a breath. I didn't let the pause last. "What did you do?"

"I had a friend ask around about buying a used computer system. Murphy was happy enough to oblige. We set up a sting, and I got some great video of the event. Murphy ended up confessing to the whole thing."

I stared at Wilson. I'm not sure which amazed me more, that the real criminal had been so easy to catch or that I hadn't thought of something along those lines to clear my name long ago.

"You just had a friend call him up?"

Wilson laughed and dropped his voice to a whisper. "Well, it wasn't quite that simple. My friend moves in the same circles as Murphy, and I had to pay him a small fee." Which suddenly made the scene in the library with Alex make perfect sense.

"Still, it was worth it," Wilson said. He glanced at Dante and then back at me. "Worth it to clear your name, I mean."

Right. I knew it had been worth it to Wilson because it had given him leverage with Jesse, and in the end with Dante too. I couldn't resent Wilson, though. With each passing moment I realized more and more ways my life had just improved. This meant no more hours of forced community service with Earl watching over my shoulder. No more probation. And best of all, people would stop making jokes about my criminal tendencies. The Frog Avenger was about to retire.

I thanked Dante on the way home, and while we sat in the kitchen with Skipper eating after-school snacks, and while he worked on his motorcycle. Pretty much I followed him around throwing out exclamations of gratitude. "I bet they'll stop making me see the school counselor too," I told him. We were out in the garage, and I was leaning up against the wall watching him polish the chrome on his bike. "From now on, no one but my parents will tell me to take responsibility for my actions."

"And you don't have to listen to them," Dante said. "Welcome back to ordinary teenage life."

I let out a happy sigh. "I can hold my head high at school again. Everyone will think I'm completely normal now—well, except for the people who know I just went out with a compulsive gambling geek who lost me to another guy on a bet."

Dante laughed, shook his head, and ran a rag over the front of his bike.

I glanced down at my cell phone, which I was still carrying around because Jesse hadn't called back yet. I knew he would, though, because he cared about me. Everyone should be as happy I was. Especially Dante. And Charity.

I watched my brother silently for a moment, wondering what he felt for her. I tried to ask in a roundabout way so he wouldn't get suspicious. "So are you going to prom?"

"No, it's too much hassle."

"Then what are you going to do on prom night?"

He picked up a fresh rag and dabbed leather cleaner onto it. "I thought I'd have a get-together over here. Maybe rent a few videos. Just something for people who don't want to do the whole dance scene. Plus, I'll invite everyone who helped out on my campaign."

Which would mean Charity. Maybe that's why he was doing it. She couldn't go to prom because of that whole no-dating-until-sixteen rule, and he wanted to be with her. Maybe. "So . . ." I let the word drift off as I scrutinized Dante for hints of his feelings. "Are you inviting anyone over that you like?"

"Don't be stupid," he said. "I don't like Raine. In fact, I'm not even inviting her."

I folded my arms, some of my good humor toward him evaporating. "I never said you liked her. You'll notice I also never said she liked you. But she did work on your campaign."

"She's going to be busy that night. Stephen asked her to prom today."

This was news. "Stephen asked her? He told you that?"

"Told me, nothing. I paid him to do it."

"You paid him to . . ." I put my hand over my eyes and shook my head. "Oh, Dante."

He glanced up at me from behind the seat of his motorcycle. "Hey, it's worth the money to set her up with someone just so I don't have to dive around corners every time I see her. And who knows? Maybe they'll hit it off."

Well, at least if he ever found out Charity liked him and he didn't like her back, she could rest assured that when she could date, he would pay one of his friends to take her out. See, there really always is a silver lining.

"Did you ask Charity to your party?"

"Sure, she worked on my campaign." He seemed far too unconcerned about this, and I couldn't tell if he really cared about the whole thing. Had he set up a get-together so he could spend time with Charity, or would it be some guy thing, and she'd end up the only one not talking about motorcycle parts?

The twin bond had failed me. I couldn't tell if he was thinking about her or not.

Dante took a step away from his bike, put his hands on his hips, and surveyed his work. "The Demonmobile is clean."

Oh yeah. He was thinking of Charity. It was bound to be a very small gathering.

My cell phone finally rang, and the next moment Jesse's voice came through the phone, warm and familiar. "Hey, can you come out front of your house for a minute?"

"Out front?" I nearly opened the garage door, but then decided if I was meeting Jesse in my front yard, I didn't want to do it with Dante watching me. There might, after all, be kissing involved. I went out the front door instead.

Out on my driveway, Jesse sat on his bike. He carried a white bakery box, and as I walked over to him, he held it out to me.

"What is it?" I asked.

"Open it and see."

I took the box from his hand and lifted the lid. Inside was a cake shaped like a pair of tennis shoes. It even had frosting shoelaces. I stared down at them. "Oh, Jesse, that is the sweetest thing . . ."

"Well, hopefully it will be. I figured it was better than making you eat your Reeboks."

I held the box close. "I get to eat my cake and have my shoes too."

He laughed, then reached over and kissed me. That's when Gabby pulled into the driveway.

She parked her car, flung open her door, and climbed out. She shook her head as she walked toward me, her expression cold. "I suppose you'll try and tell me that Jesse is here visiting Dante again."

I opened my mouth to explain, but she held up one hand to stop me. "You're not officially ungrounded until tomorrow. Although now I wonder if that date is premature."

Then she stormed past me, slamming the door as she went inside.

Which, I suppose, meant Dante was halfway to getting his Corvette.

Jesse let out a ragged sigh. "Sorry to get you in trouble. I guess I'd better go."

"I'll call you later," I said, then watched him drive off.

It was just my luck to get grounded again right when Jesse and I got back together.

I went inside, walking toward the kitchen to put away the cake, but stopped when I heard Dante and Gabby's voices coming from there.

"Yeah, I came in third place," Dante said dejectedly.

"Third?" Gabby asked. "But I thought there were only two candidates."

Dante let out a sigh. "It started out that way, but at the last minute a lot of people decided to vote for a write-in."

Gabby gasped. "That doesn't sound fair."

Another sigh from Dante. "I guess the kids at school just don't think I'm cool enough. Maybe if I had my own car . . ."

I turned and walked to my room instead. He was so shameless.

When my dad came home, they sat me down in the living room for the big lecture. Gabby said that she wanted to trust me, but no, I just kept breaking the rules, and what sort of future was I going to have with that attitude?

I heard it unemotionally, almost like she spoke to someone else. I'm not sure why. Maybe because Jesse and I were back together again. Maybe because I was still so amazed at what Dante and Jesse and even Wilson had done for me. Gabby simply couldn't chip away any of my goodwill.

I looked at her and said, "It's a funny thing about my future. You'll never guess what happened." But I couldn't start right there. I had to start at the beginning. So I told them how Jesse had been Wilson's campaign manager and I'd fought with him and yelled, "We're over!" in front of everybody, and then I'd regretted it, but it was too late. I told them everything. This big torrential downpour of words just came out of my mouth.

I told them that Jesse had been trying to help me all

along and Dante had quit the election for me, and at this moment my future looked pretty good because I had been cleared of everything.

And the strangest thing happened. Gabby had sat perfectly still all through my story, but when I told her the part about what Jesse and Dante had done, she teared up, put her fingers to her lips, and said, "That's so wonderful. Now you won't have to worry about college or job applications."

She said more, mostly about Dante, but the words she'd said to me turned around and around in my mind until I was very sure she'd actually said them.

Something good had happened to me, and it made her happy. I know that shouldn't seem strange, but I'd almost expected her to be disappointed. Like, she wanted to rub in all of my mistakes, and if there was one less that she could pick out of her You're-a-lousy-kid bag, she'd be upset. But she was glad for me.

Dad called Dante into the living room, and then the whole thing turned into this huge praise-fest for Dante.

He just smiled and said, "It wasn't really a big deal," which of course made my parents praise him all the more.

He was so getting a car soon, and I just hoped he let me drive it once in a while.

My parents also decided not to be angry that Jesse

had come over to bring me a cake. Gabby even said, "We should invite him over for dinner soon. How about Sunday evening?"

So that was basically it. I had stumbled upon something here, though I wasn't exactly sure what. All I had done was tell them what was going on in my life. Was it really as simple as that? Was that all I needed to do to put Gabby on my side?

It was definitely worth considering.

On Sunday I helped Gabby make chicken scarpariello for dinner, which felt weirdly like mother-daughter bonding time. When Dante wandered into the kitchen, Gabby made him set the table. "Use the good dishes," she told him.

Dante lugged them out of the china hutch, grumbling. "So Jesse's coming over. I'm the one who conceded the election. You guys never get the good dishes out for me."

Poor him.

Gabby ignored Dante and put the chicken into the oven. "I just wish there was some way we could thank Wilson. Do you think we should send him a card—or maybe bake him something?"

Dante went to the silverware drawer and grabbed a handful of forks. "I didn't set his palm trees on fire. I think that's thanks enough."

Later on, Jesse came over, and we all had a nice meal together, despite the fact that Skipper kept interrupting the conversation to tell us new words she'd learned—which probably meant at some point Dante had been dangerously close to swearing.

After dinner I walked Jesse outside to his bike, and we stood talking.

"So you're not grounded anymore?"

"Apparently not." I took his hand in mine, gently swinging it. "Because I've learned my lesson."

"What was the lesson?"

"If I'm nice to Gabby, she's way more lenient with her punishments."

Jesse laughed. His eyes twinkled. I could just stare at him and never get tired of it. "So I can ask you to prom now?"

"Yes," I said. "And yes, I'll go with you."

"Good." He bent down and gave me a kiss, which not only stopped time but momentarily changed the course of the sun until it revolved around us. When he finally let me go and said good-bye, I could still feel its warmth all around me.

I watched him get on his bike and drive away, then I turned around to go inside.

I was going to prom. And more importantly, I was going to prom with Jesse. A voice in my mind that sounded remarkably like Dante's said, "If you ask Gabby to go gown shopping with you, she'll pay for the dress." Which went to show you that our twin bond was working—well, either that or I was starting to think like Dante.

I laughed and went inside.